"A meditation on vanity, the ways in which the pursuit of physical beauty can betray the other sources of beauty in one's life, and how horror can lurk beneath the surface of even the most poreless skin." —Jazmine Hughes, *The New York Times Book Review*

"Absorbing . . . *Natural Beauty* starts out frothy, offering an enticing dip into how tech could beautify and perfect our bodies and faces in the near future. . . . It quickly veers into subversive horror, turning into a cautionary tale on societal themes we're currently seeing IRL." —*Vogue*

"A must-read . . . We'd recommend it to anyone intrigued by girlboss discourse, sci-fi, love triangles, mysteries, and injectables, or who has ever thought, *What if there was an episode of* Black Mirror *inspired by Goop?*" —SELF

"A thriller mixed with horror and laced with a biting dose of social commentary, *Natural Beauty* is a book you won't be able to stop thinking about." —*Glamour*

"This is a darkly absurd and hilarious skewering of the luxury beauty industry, as well as a heart-wrenching story of a woman left alone in the world." —*BuzzFeed*

"Goop-core body horror . . . *Natural Beauty* is a delightfully baroque grotesque. It can achieve a folkloric power in its creepiest moments—a scary story you'd tell in a posh spa's sauna instead of around a campfire."
—*Wired*

"Insidious Western standards, fears about bodily autonomy, and queer desire intersect as Huang's precise and subtle portrayal of the beauty industry builds to an explosive climax. Alternatingly poignant and deeply unsettling, this is an outstanding first outing for an immensely talented author."
—*Publishers Weekly* (starred review)

"Haunting and immersive . . . The writing is lyrical even when plot events are profoundly tragic, and the protagonist's journey will captivate readers throughout."
—*Booklist* (starred review)

"*Natural Beauty* is a horror novel that digs deep into the evils of exploitative industries."
—Shondaland

"*Natural Beauty* uses elements of sci-fi, fantasy, and body horror to cut to bone-deep truths about consumerism, race, identity, appearance, and the exhausting pursuit of perfection."
—Jessica DeFino, The Unpublishable

"Eerie and entertaining . . . Ling Ling Huang is a fearless storyteller, and this book is as luminous as it is thrilling."
—Pik-Shuen Fung, author of *Ghost Forest*

"Ling Ling Huang amplifies and expands the future of horror fiction with a book so riveting it is impossible to put down."
—Rikki Ducornet, author of *Phosphor in Dreamland*

"A modern-day *Picture of Dorian Gray* shot through a Cronenbergian lens, Ling Ling Huang's *Natural Beauty* has big things to say about art, society, and the obsessive pursuit of youth."
— Nick Cutter, author of *The Troop*, *The Deep*, and *Little Heaven*

"Huang frets the 'fine line between beauty and ugliness, ripeness and rot' in this alluring tale of estrangement, body horror, and possibly a new genre, Dark Wellness—pierced through by a daughter's love for her immigrant parents. Ardent and unsettling."
— Lisa Hsiao Chen, author of *Activities of Daily Living*

"A surreal, dreamlike thriller . . . The cinematic storytelling shows what happens when businesses trade on the most extreme levels of human desires. Gripping!"
— Frances Cha, author of *If I Had Your Face*

"Precise, unflinching, and utterly unforgettable, *Natural Beauty* is both a razor-sharp critique of the beauty industry and a startlingly tender story of family and sacrifice. This book will swallow you whole."
— Grace D. Li, *New York Times* bestselling author of *Portrait of a Thief*

"A propulsive, captivating read, *Natural Beauty* pulled me into its world like a fever dream. A prescient look at the dirty underbelly of society's beauty standards, it also carries a moving reminder that true beauty is often found in the very things we've been taught to abandon."
— Constance Wu, star of *Crazy Rich Asians* and author of *Making a Scene*

NATURAL BEAUTY

a novel

LING LING HUANG

DUTTON

DUTTON

An imprint of Penguin Random House LLC
penguinrandomhouse.com

Previously published as a Dutton hardcover in April 2023
First Dutton trade paperback printing: April 2024
Copyright © 2023 by Ling Ling Huang
Penguin Random House supports copyright. Copyright fuels creativity, encourages
diverse voices, promotes free speech, and creates a vibrant culture. Thank you for buying
an authorized edition of this book and for complying with copyright laws by not reproducing,
scanning, or distributing any part of it in any form without permission. You are supporting
writers and allowing Penguin Random House to continue to publish books for every reader.

DUTTON and the D colophon are registered trademarks of
Penguin Random House LLC.

THE LIBRARY OF CONGRESS HAS CATALOGED THE HARDCOVER EDITION OF THIS BOOK AS FOLLOWS:

Names: Huang, Ling Ling, 1989– author.
Title: Natural beauty : a novel / Ling Ling Huang.
Description: New York : Dutton, [2023]
Identifiers: LCCN 2022027633 (print) | LCCN 2022027634 (ebook) |
ISBN 9780593472927 (hardcover) | ISBN 9780593472934 (ebook)
Subjects: LCGFT: Black humor. | Satirical literature. | Novels.
Classification: LCC PS3608.U22483 N38 2023 (print) |
LCC PS3608.U22483 (ebook) | DDC 813/.6—dc23/eng/20220819
LC record available at https://lccn.loc.gov/2022027633
LC ebook record available at https://lccn.loc.gov/2022027634

Dutton trade paperback ISBN: 9780593472941

Printed in the United States of America
1st Printing

Interior art: Pattern © giterichka / Shutterstock

BOOK DESIGN BY KRISTIN DEL ROSARIO

For my parents

NATURAL BEAUTY

CHAPTER ONE

Even the door is beautiful. A single piece of dark heavy wood, like rich chocolate poured under an ancient stone archway carved with wings and scales. My hand rests on the golden doorknob, surprisingly hot to the touch. A twist and a push and I am pulled in by the deep pink carpets and the soft muted clinking of expensive products. Warm candlelight emanates from every surface. A light botanical smell fills the air.

People mill around, tightly wrapped in sumptuous wools and furs. They sniff, drip, and dribble substances onto themselves. Light gray mother-of-pearl inlays stripe the walls. When the light catches, they seem to move like the sudden falling of tears. In fact, the entire place feels unusually alive, as if I have stumbled into the womb of a slumbering giantess.

In the back, a tall man in a sharp black suit stands next to a woman caressing the sleeping sloth curled around her neck. He nods at her a few times before crouching down abruptly to catch a vial tumbling from a toddler's pudgy hand. He straightens and smiles at the child as he places the product out of reach. He moves with authority, towering over everyone. Balletic and rigorous in his economy of movement.

His dark blond hair is slicked close to his head, and his face has a rubbery quality, like it would hold a pressed handprint. The exception is his cheekbones, which slice the air like fins. I realize he looks familiar, though I can't remember where I've seen him. The wall behind him is light pink, filled with rows and rows of white ceramic jars, like gleaming teeth embedded in a healthy set of gums.

"Darling, you came! Welcome to Holistik."

Saje walks over with quick steps and slips an arm through mine. I worry that she can smell me, the November air not yet cold enough to keep me from sweating on my long walk here. Her smile is warm. "What do you think?"

She's wearing a silky nude jumpsuit, and dark red hair snakes over her shoulder, glinting in the dim lighting. Her irises are brown but have a surprising yellow edge I hadn't noticed last night. She is so tall in her animal-skin stilettos, I have to strain my neck to meet her eye.

"Would you be interested in working here?"

My jaw drops open and my mouth fills with cold air. I hastily shut it, embarrassed, and look at her for a few long seconds to see if there's any chance she's fucking with me. Her expression is unchanged—and looking around at all the products, so many specifically made to keep women from ever aging, I wonder if she's even capable of different expressions.

"Yes," I say, exalting her by craning my neck as high as it will go. She starts to explain the particulars of the job, the pay and benefits included, and I feel a wave of relief so intense, I have to reach out and grab the display table next to me.

"Thank you," I add, surprised to find myself blinking back tears.

Her smile widens, showing teeth. "No thanks necessary. I'm so glad I found you. I knew from the moment we met that you'd be the perfect addition to our little family here. I'll introduce you to Lilith in a moment. She'll be the one to show you around. Why don't you go downstairs? There's an employee closet where you can put your things."

CHAPTER TWO

take the stairs down and pause. How different from my previous place of employment. Every bit as opulent as the floor above, this private space is enormous and inviting. A few women seem to float together on a cloudlike structure that acts as a sofa. They are homogeneously beautiful, as if airlifted from a movie set about popular high school girls. They are still in character, perhaps, since they don't acknowledge or even notice me. Gigantic shelves loom on the left, crammed with stone jars and crystal vials. A clean, faintly medicinal smell puts me at ease. It is cold down here, refreshingly so, and I love the clinical click of my shoes on the porcelain tiles.

The full kitchen is spotless, as if it has never been used. My view through the clear refrigerator door is blocked by a dense forest of rainbow-colored juices. I ignore my sudden hunger pangs and begin my search for the employee closet.

I pass a door with an electronic lock. A sign over it: *The Zoo*. Down the main hallway, a glass door. Beyond it, people dressed in white lab coats move with urgency. On a table in front of them, something wrinkled and translucent pumps like a beating heart.

Jellyfish, I think, though they look like crumpled plastic bags recently fished out of water. In the closet, I leave my bag and hang up my ratty old coat. At least the clothes I am wearing underneath are somewhat nicer. Long sleeves, as Saje had requested.

She had stomped in late, looking so filthy rich no one wanted to tell her the restaurant was closed. She was very beautiful, with skin so white it was almost translucent, and her long red hair was tucked into a lavender coat that looked incredibly soft. I could have believed someone was airbrushing her live image.

I had just finished another day of scrubbing endless dishes in piping hot water. It wasn't so bad once I'd gotten used to it. At the end of each night, I would kick off my shoes, eat leftovers from the kitchen, and strip the burned skin from my hands. I felt triumphant when I could get a large piece off all at once, like peeling off an opera glove. Months of lightly flaying myself had made the raw skin baby soft, and I sometimes fantasized about submerging my whole body in the sink, shedding everything.

"May I have one?" She slipped into the seat opposite mine, gesturing at my leftovers, coiling her legs beneath her.

I masked my surprise with politeness. "Sure. They're cold, though."

She picked at the soggy fries, pushing them through a small opening between her two front teeth. I was mesmerized by this action. The gap caused a soft musical whistle when she spoke, as if she had songbirds in her throat. She sighed and the birds took flight. I felt grimy sitting across from her, surely exuding the smell of recycled frying oil from every orifice.

"Man's greatest invention, don't you think? The potato with salt," the woman said, licking a finger.

I said nothing. Carla was glaring at me from behind the counter, prematurely accusing me of stealing a wealthy customer.

"Did you know that they can be toxic? Nothing serious. You won't die from a potato, but it can make you very ill," she said.

I smiled reflexively. Rich people have all the time in the world to pick up random anecdotes for small talk.

She suddenly leaned in, peering at me with an inquisitiveness that made me stop breathing. "Wait a minute. I know you."

I almost looked behind me. "Excuse me?"

"You look very familiar. Have we met?"

I gazed at her once more, carefully, before shaking my head. My hair, greasy from a day next to the fryer, didn't move.

"Have you been in the city a long time? Do you study here?"

Close enough, I thought as I nodded.

"What do you study?"

"I studied piano. At the Conservatory."

There was a look of recognition on her face.

She jabbed a fry at me. "I knew it. You're her! The Rachmaninoff girl!" she said. "Am I right?"

A quick nod.

"You're incredible! I love the piano, and I'm a huge supporter of the arts!"

"That's great," I say.

There's a pause before I realize I should thank her for supporting the vague "arts," which in this instance is me. "Thanks so much."

"What are you doing here? A bit far from the Conservatory, aren't you?" She was leaning in so close, I could feel her hot breath on my face.

"I'm not there anymore."

"Where are you playing next? I would love to see you perform."

I hesitated, still unsure of how to answer these types of questions. It had been almost three years since I had touched a piano. For a second, I imagined shrinking in size and bouncing on her fully cushioned lips instead of answering her.

"I don't really play anymore."

"You don't? Why!"

"It was just time to move on."

"How do you make a living?"

"I work here. Dishwasher." I showed her my hands.

Predictably, she gasped.

"But what a waste of your hands! Your talent!"

I shrugged.

"They must pay a fortune if that's what you're doing to yourself!"

"It's better than nothing. I get a lot of free food."

Before the restaurant job, I consistently found myself choosing between eating enough and putting money away for rent. I never went through with it, but there were too many nights when I waited for my roommates to fall asleep before creeping upstairs to listen to the quiet burbling of their cat's triple-filtered water fountain and to stand transfixed by the gleam of gold tops on her gourmet cat food.

"Stop by anytime. Ask for me." She was opening her purse and reaching inside. "I go to the Philharmonic every week, and I've never heard a pianist who can do what you do. You deserve better, and we can certainly give you more than free food."

I was startled to see a look of genuine concern in her eyes. The card she slid onto the sticky tabletop was iridescent and embossed with the word *Holistik*. The script was so lavishly curled, the letters looked like they might sneak off the card to ensnare me. She turned it around and tapped on her name a couple of times.

Saje Bernsson.

She rose, encompassing me in her shadow. "My driver is waiting." She placed a cold hand over one of mine, shocking me. "I hope to see you soon." Putting leather gloves on at the door, she looked back at me, remembering something. "Wear long sleeves when you visit."

The wind let in a flurry of freshly fallen leaves, red as her hair. Feathers, too, inexplicably floated out from her open handbag. They swirled in the wind, eventually sticking to the dirty tile.

I find a bathroom across from the employee closet. The floor is spongy, and every step emits a whiff of something sublime. It appears to be a carpet made of woven eucalyptus, matted and pulverized to be plush and springy underfoot. A tub lined with jars of scented salts takes up half the room. I slip into the large celadon half egg, opening the carafes and smelling each one, almost compulsively. My bladder is full, but I can't imagine using the toilet, which looks like an art piece. In the mirror, I'm surprised to find that the soft light makes me look well rested. Not quite beautiful, but not completely out of place in this enchanted setting. A creamy soap is dispensed from a sculpture of a bathing woman, and I sink my hands into a dense fluffy towel before hurrying back upstairs.

Saje is waiting for me near the stairs with a strikingly beautiful young woman. A light gray gauze, more mist than coat, is draped over her tight-knit dress and over-the-knee leather boots. She has long glossy hair the color of roasting chestnuts and dark green eyes with all the depth and chill of an overgrown forest. She can't be much older than I am, but on her face, there is more than a hint of superiority. I don't yet know this to be a trait shared by all Holistik girls.

"There you are! This is Lilith. She's our exceptional manager, and she'll tell you everything you need to know."

"Hi," I say, anxious under Lilith's cool gaze.

She dips her chin slightly in my direction as a greeting. "Are you headed back to the Gunks?" she asks Saje, who answers affirmatively before turning back to me.

"I am so happy you're joining us. A quick word before I leave?" Saje asks.

I glance nervously at Lilith. She covers a yawn with a tiny hand before stepping two paces away.

Saje's eyes glow with pleasure as she looks me up and down. "You already fit in so beautifully. As you can see, we favor an international staff."

I look around, but none of the other staff seem particularly international to me. If anything, I seem like a clear diversity hire. I lower my head in agreement like a good model minority.

"I want to warn you about some of our customers. They may assume you're from the Mainland or another country. It's offensive, especially in this day and age, but it might be best to let them think they're right and to focus on the products you're selling."

I try to smile.

"Exactly like that. And do bring up the formal piano training. Only if you're comfortable, of course. We have a few expensive hand creams that may sell especially well with your endorsement." She reaches over and squeezes my shoulder. "That reminds me." She pops a little glass jar into my palm. "For your poor hands. I'll see you soon! Lilith will take great care of you." She walks away, leaving me alone with Lilith.

I look at the jar, unscrew the heavy lid, and dab a bit on my left hand. A light floral scent rises as the thick cream clings to my skin. Nothing like the watery stuff Ma would rub on my aching hands after long sessions of piano practice. She fortified cheap lotion or Vaseline with a liniment she made using Chinese herbs. Every night after dinner, no matter how exhausted she was, she would soften the calluses on my fingertips so they wouldn't split open. We would watch TV, I would read to her from a book, or she would tell me the things she missed about home. We always drank chrysanthemum tea, steeping the same tired flowers from the day before. The fingers of one hand would always run impatiently while she massaged the other one.

"You're just like me," Ma said. "Every morning in Cultural Revolution, we woke up and officers watch us carefully make sure we read the Little Red Book. I always keep my fingers moving. So small they can't see. But moving. Hope one day get out, can play piano again."

"She was his mistress," Lilith says coolly.

She had seen my eyes glazing over at the memory of my mother and assumed it was a reaction to the microscopic print on her translucent shawl. I look closer, focusing this time on the delicate name tag. Her eyes blink slowly at me with boredom as if to say, *Yes, I am the child of that famous director. No, I wasn't conceived in something as ordinary as marriage.*

"The lab downstairs will want to get samples from you and take measurements for your uniform. It shouldn't take more than fifteen minutes. Come find me on the floor afterward."

I make my way back downstairs.

People in white lab coats run around, scanning and swabbing me with whirring devices.

"What's all of this for?" I ask the nearest young man.

"We're testing the composition of your body and facial skin to make custom products and supplements for you. They'll be ready at the end of your shift today. One of the many perks of working here."

He grins and continues circling my head with a protracted gray rod. I imagine him bringing it down on me repeatedly.

Next he brings me to a small room by the lab where he tells me my new Holistik uniform will be constructed. Another man sprays me with something before I enter, and the taste catches in my throat, faintly floral like jasmine tea, but mostly sticky.

"Semiochemicals for the worms. You're not afraid of worms, are you?"

In the room, I clear my throat to try and get it to unstick. The man gives me a thumbs-up from a little window. One by one, they start to descend. The room I had thought was empty is filled with thousands of worms, lowering from the ceiling on delicate string. They twist and somersault drunk figure eights. The sound of silk being spun is beautiful, a silvery hum with an indiscernible pitch. My mind can't help but try to transcribe it into music I can play. Suddenly, the little bleached bodies begin to retract, and a voice speaks over an intercom.

"You can come through the door now."

I hesitate and look back. A gentle wind starts blowing in the room and I begin to feel faint. A hand grabs me—the man with the rod earlier has opened the door. His hand is warm and too tight around my wrist, as if I've done something wrong.

"It's all right, you're OK!" He steadies me and I try to blink away the white spots in my eyes. I feel sure that without his support, I would fall.

"What's happening to me?"

"You're OK," he says firmly. "Just a little cross-contamination. Something we use for the worms to make them obedient. For the silk extraction."

I look back through the window at the dangling silkworms. "Are they—"

He waves a hand impatiently. "They're OK. They're paralyzed for a bit while we extract and shape the silk, but they'll continue their life cycle afterward. The alternative is boiling them alive, so I think they would agree this is preferable. Even if they had memories, they wouldn't remember a thing."

He looks at me with his brows knitted together.

"I'll walk you upstairs," he says.

Through the little window, I watch as the air inside the room grows perceptibly stronger, blowing the silkworms until they fall en masse to the ground, a sudden shower of snow.

Lilith hands me a thick deck of illustrated cards as soon as I get upstairs. I flip one over. A long bell-shaped flower. *Borrachero tree* is written underneath, with a list of products and applications. The next card features a watercolor of golden wattles. The brushstrokes are so delicate I have to restrain myself from trying to lift the wattle's delicate fluff off the page.

"Think of these as take-home flashcards for our products," she says.

Hundreds of products, it turns out. Creams, powders, serums, cleansers, oils, dry oils, drips, essences, acids, toners. A never-ending treasure trove of human ingenuity. Each with unique ingredients, targeted benefits, and very specific application methods. As Lilith gives me a tour, my head spins with new information and my skin stings from trying all the products. By the end of the day, one of my cheeks is bouncy and soft, the other taut. My nose runs from an allergic reaction and my lips swell from a sticky gloss.

"You look beautiful!" a customer remarks as I pass her.

"Thank you," I struggle to say through numb lips.

"It's the venom," Lilith reassures me.

I look at her in alarm.

"From the Japanese mamushi. A pit viper." She laughs at my reaction. "Don't worry, the dosage is very precise."

Her laugh catches me off guard. Her beauty is severe and her expression serious, but when she laughs, her cheeks become rosy and full except for a small indentation in the right cheek. I imagine dipping my pinky toe into her dimple.

We pass a display case of empty glass jars, each one priced at several hundred dollars.

"What are these?"

She glances at them. "Snake food."

I look from the empty jars to her equally blank face and back again. "There's nothing in them."

"Well, it's not physical food. It's spiritual food to awaken Kundalini, the power serpent of divine energy that lives at the base of our spine."

A small silver pebble hanging on a delicate strand around Lilith's neck begins to hum. I stare in surprise. The vibration increases until it lifts slightly from her neck. She wraps her hand around the object and slips it off the chain. It swings open with a swift movement of her fingers, and she removes a handful of what look like tiny precious jewels, transferring them to her mouth.

"That reminds me," she says, pulling a velvet pouch out of a pocket. "Hold out your hand."

She extracts a lump of clear putty from the bag and dumps it onto my palm. It prickles a bit as it lands and hardens until it becomes identical to the pebble around her neck. I turn it over and over, trying to figure out how it achieved such a dramatic transformation.

"Beautiful, aren't they? We all have one. They're designed by Matthieu Ricard and powered by Avidia Tech. It's basically a physical Holistik app. It'll remind you when to take your supplements, and you can keep the most important ones inside so they're readily accessible."

"The pills and stuff are required?" Saje hadn't mentioned anything about this earlier.

"Along with monthly facials, massages, and skin treatments. The more experimental stuff is optional. Encouraged . . . but not mandatory. Some of the girls definitely take it too far, in my opinion." Her hands drop from my neck after she helps me put on my new accessory. The chain cinches suddenly and clasps on its own. She peers at a tiny gold watch on her wrist and frowns, pulling her hair back with an elastic. "We have to set up for a procedure."

I follow Lilith down a long dark hallway into the spa wing. Her pert ponytail and bangs bounce rhythmically as she walks, reminding me of the metronome I used for piano practice as a child. Most of the doors are open, and my eyes take in sumptuous massage beds, steam rooms, and bright aqua whirlpools. When we step inside the last room of the hallway, I react with a loud gasp before I can stop myself. Lilith rolls her eyes as I recoil from the door.

"I know. It smells foul, but you'll get used to it."

There is a large gleaming tub in the corner and three wooden crates on the floor. Lilith pins her thick bangs to one side before opening a drawer and removing two sets of tongs. I take the pair she hands me.

"Ready?" Lilith pries off the lid of a box and hundreds of crabs scuttle out. "We toss them in there."

She works fast, panting as she picks up and deposits crabs into the tub with her tongs. I try to match her speed, but they are unwieldy and strong. The stench is unbearable, reminding me of the time the walk-in freezer stopped working at the restaurant. I was tasked with disposing of the catfish fillets, which had rotted and slimed together. I carried them in schools down the block to the dumpster and my fingernails smelled of fish for weeks.

The last crate is smaller, containing only a few fish.

"Remora," Lilith says, slowly lowering them into the tub.

"What kind of procedure is this?"

Lilith stops for a moment and stares at me with narrowed eyes. "You've never heard of the Chaoshan Mud Treatment."

"No."

"The procedure that launched a thousand copycat treatments."

"To be honest, I just learned about Holistik yesterday."

Lilith looks doubtful. "But you probably saw Victor, right?"

"I'm not sure. What does he look like?"

"You don't know what Victor Carroll looks like?"

"No."

"He's tall. He was wearing a black suit."

"Oh, yes, I saw him."

"Victor is the owner and CEO of Organic Provisions, the parent company of Holistik."

"*He's* the owner? Not Saje?"

"Saje is the face of Holistik, but Victor is the one who makes the decisions. Optically, it's better right now to have a female founder and owner. Drives a lot more revenue."

"Right."

"You've really never heard of Victor Carroll."

"No."

"Youngest *Forbes* 30 Under 30."

"No."

"Founder of Avidia Tech? Genysis Models, Psy-stems?"

I shake my head.

"Wow. Did you grow up under a rock?"

CHAPTER THREE

Not a rock exactly, but a room consisting of only myself and a piano, for the better part of my twenty-three years. Ma and Ba were both pianists, poised for success until the Cultural Revolution disrupted their lives. They were among the fortunate who were sent to labor camps instead of being executed or harassed to commit suicide.

When the Cultural Revolution ended, they applied for scholarships at American schools, eager to escape the country that had torn apart so many families and lives. Though his once masterful fingers had only touched root vegetables and mud for three years, Ba was accepted by a school in New York, and Ma was allowed to go with him. They arrived in America alone, in their early twenties, with little money and no comprehension of the English language. Despite the many barriers they faced, they worked hard and dreamed of owning a piano one day.

When he wasn't struggling through the impenetrable English terminology used in music theory and musicology classes, Ba stood outside of grocery stores and asked people for jobs while Ma worked as a nanny for several families. Because they didn't know how to read English, they couldn't look for employment in newspaper ads and relied solely on referrals. Ba was able to find enough odd jobs for a small but steady stream of income.

Ma had a more difficult time getting referrals because of her reputation as a bad cook. Before she learned how to drown everything in ketchup, she was often let go because her young charges complained to their parents about the food she made for them.

By the time I was born, they were both piano teachers, taking turns teaching students all day on the piano in our small house. I begged to play also, but they wanted a different life for me. I was pushed to study hard in school so I wouldn't end up like them, two piano teachers in the same house: rich in sound and nothing else. Every day, I woke and fell asleep to their teaching. Anything from the most complex Prokofiev sonatas to the drudgery beginning students practiced.

I also heard the music they played for each other and for themselves, late at night when I was supposed to be asleep. One night, I crept out of my room for a closer listen.

"Where do you want to go today?" Ba asked.

My ears pricked. Where could my parents be going at this hour?

Ma laughed. "Czech Republic?"

Ba played something on the piano.

"Germany?"

Ba played a lick from another piece.

Ma laughed again. Knowing they weren't going anywhere without me, I relaxed and tiptoed back to bed.

Music began to give me anxiety. Where did all the notes go? Thousands of notes echoed in our cramped house, accumulating, crowding. I started dreaming that my bones were made of sound. I felt them crawling into my head at night, clinging to my skin, wanting to find pulse in my blood. I found the houses of other people strange. How did they live with such silence? Some mornings, I didn't think I could get out of bed without someone striking a chord, summoning or even constructing me.

My parents gave in when I was six and started teaching me piano. The notes that had crowded in me flowed from my hands. I was overjoyed to finally learn the language in which my parents communicated most deeply.

I progressed at a rapid speed, showing exceptional promise, though by most standards six is far too late to begin any instrument. Ma despaired to see me so attached to the thing that had caused such loss in her life before it saved her. I could feel her watching me with a question in her eyes when I practiced. Neither of my parents could understand my love for the instrument, a love that seemed to outweigh their own.

"It's as if she were the one forced to stop playing for years," I once overheard Ma telling her sister on the phone.

I did love piano, but as a means, not an end. When my parents played, the instrument fell away. Ma put her fingers to the keys and flowers bloomed in fragrant sound. When Ba played, it was as if through the mist over a river, the piano bench creaking beneath him like an oar. I wanted the same power of expression.

After I ate dinner, I would practice on the little keyboard in

my room as I waited for my parents to finish their lessons. Then
we would watch TV together while they ate their dinner. Ma
especially loved TV. It was her preferred method of learning English while Ba made his way steadily through my grade school
workbooks. We ended every evening the same way. Ba asked us
where we wanted to go and transported us there. Their favorite
place to go was home. Ma would shake her head shyly when Ba
played the songs that had been popular when he and Ma were
growing up. Songs that depicted the country people often told
me to return to, but that I had never seen. Ma always sang along
softly and I would try to follow, but my tongue snarled on the
difficult syllables. My parents never looked as happy and as sad
as when they were singing the songs from their youth. I often
wondered in these moments what it cost them to never show
fragility. Only determination and resilience in the face of their
new country. In the silence between notes, I began to hear the
wound my parents hid from me. I learned the songs by ear, and
within a few weeks, I was able to play them. Music was the suturing that connected them to their home and I finally had a part in
the healing of our family.

   Ba had fewer reservations about my interest in the piano. He
was thrilled with my progress and splurged on a digital camcorder so that I could film my daily practice sessions and he could
listen to how I was doing after his long days of teaching. He up-
loaded my practice sessions onto the internet for his friends and
family in China. They saw a piece of our lives in America. A
room with a piano and the daughter who didn't need to work and
had time for school and music. They made assumptions, not
knowing that it took months for our finances to recover from the
purchase of the camcorder. I always had the same amount of food

on my plate, but my parents went with considerably less. They continued to give me the few cubes of pork or fish we could afford while they ate only rice and the leaves of sweet potato plants. It was the first time I learned that to love is to go hungry.

Thousands of viewers tuned in from all over the world and I became an internet sensation. I received invitations to St. Petersburg and Vienna and Budapest, to study with the best teachers in Europe. The Berlin Academy offered me an unprecedented scholarship. And the Conservatory professors in New York City made a house visit to meet the little Chinese girl who was embarrassing them by sweeping the local competitions, beating out all their students.

I was practicing a new piece when the cars—too nice to belong to any of the families my parents taught—pulled up outside. I was offered a full scholarship, free housing, and even a generous yearly stipend, paid by an anonymous benefactor.

I was excited, impatient even, to get to the city. I would be able to help my parents by giving them a large portion of my stipend, and I wouldn't be too far from them. When I missed them, I could play piano and remember they were more than close: they were part of me.

Ma packed a small suitcase for my belongings. Clothes, sheet music, as many packs of ramen and microwaveable rice as we had, her special liniment, and, lastly, a picture of the three of us. Ba had to handwrite some of my music because the print was too minuscule for me to read at a young age. As Ma packed the music, the notes started distorting on the page. Her tears caused the black circles of ink to bleed into each other. She tried to smile when she saw me watching her.

That night, we had dinner together. A rare occasion because

of their usual teaching schedule. The piano was played so often that they never covered it. Tonight, however, a dusty red cloth hid the black and white teeth.

"One last trip?" I asked Ba.

He shook his head gently but firmly. "Tomorrow big day. They come very early take you. We all need sleep soon."

I didn't answer, but that night I snuck out of my room when I heard the piano being played. It was comforting to know that my parents would still be together every night in our music room, even if I wasn't there.

Ba was playing something exquisitely beautiful. A piece unlike anything I had ever heard. I walked toward it as if in a trance.

"You should be sleeping!" Ma said when she saw me, but I wasn't listening to her.

"What are you playing, Ba?" I looked at the piece of music in front of him and saw lines for four instruments.

"String quartet?" I looked at him with confusion.

He smiled excitedly. "I do my best transcribe for piano."

I looked at the name of the piece. "'Cavatina.' A song?"

Ba nodded and pointed to the ceiling. "It playing up there. On the Golden Record."

We were both silent for a moment, as if to listen for the music spinning in the galaxy.

"What does this word mean?" I pointed at an italicized word near the end of the page.

Beklemmt.

Ba scratched his head slowly as if reluctant to answer. "It mean choking. Heavy heart."

He sighed, his giant hands folding like cranes in his lap.

"Can you play it for me?" I whispered.

He started from the beginning. A plaintive hymn spread from the piano to the rest of the room, warming the space. There was a searching quality to the piece. All four voices restlessly trying to find one another like tree roots seeking nutrients. His sturdy hands struggled over the keys, adding to the unresolved quality of the music. The beklemmt section confused me. It wasn't what I expected.

"It doesn't sound sad to me . . . it sounds almost happy," I said to him afterward.

Ba turned to me with a frightening look on his face. There were tears in his eyes as he dragged the corners of his lips upward. "I *am* happy."

An older girl was given the assignment of showing me around. When we arrived at my new room, I took in the modest bunk bed with a stained mattress, the wood table etched with carvings, and the used scratchy blanket.

"This is all mine?"

In my first studio class at the Conservatory, a teenage boy played for an audience of classmates and teachers. I listened with my eyes closed. Studio class was a revelation. So many different works and interpretations, explored as a group in a new concert hall they told us was ours.

A professor interrupted him. "No, no, it's all wrong." His eyes found mine in the audience. "You played this for your audition, didn't you? Can you come up and play this section?"

The piece was one of my favorites, something Ba and I had worked on together a few years ago. I could hear him singing along and feel the warmth of his hands over mine, lending me the weight I needed for a sustained sound.

"*That* is how it's done," Professor Zsaborsky said when I had played to the end. "Can you tell us what you're thinking about when you play this section?"

I stared at him, not understanding. No one had ever asked me to clarify that which I had made perfectly clear through music.

"I'm thinking about how the notes in the left hand whirl like leaves in the wind, like how they chatter." I circled my left hand at the wrist a few times as if to show everyone. "And the right hand goes along with it until—" I stopped, nervous. Struggling to express my feelings about the end of the piece. I started over, remembering what Ba had told me about the piece.

"The piece is like a day. Nothing special about it . . . maybe it's even kind of boring. You're finishing your chores when you catch your reflection in the window and suddenly remember that you and everyone you love will die. It's a lonely feeling, but it comes with a weird kind of happiness, too. Like at least everyone else is feeling the same. In this huge world, we're all small together. That's why the piece feels so universal, because it's personal."

I stopped speaking, somewhat satisfied with how I had summed up Ba's feelings. Everyone in the hall was silent.

"Well, yes. That's really wonderful, but I meant, why did you choose to start with the second finger instead of the first, which is standard?"

A few of the girls in the audience tittered. I didn't know what to say. I hadn't known there was a standard fingering for the piece.

"It's just what my ba taught me," I said.

Professor Zsaborsky nodded. "And your sound. There's something peculiar about it."

I bounced nervously onstage. "Bad?" The word echoed around me, chiding me.

"No. I think it's good. Maybe very good. Just unusual."

I knew he was talking about the secret technique my parents had taught me.

"Do you know why oboe player tunes whole orchestra?" Ba had asked me when I first started piano.

I shook my head.

"Because there is edge to oboe. Up close, sounds ugly, but in bigger room, edge is extra power! Cause lot of sound and resonance! We can copy on piano. At end of every note, we curve finger and scratch with nail or fingertip. The fast motion, the small nail scratch, give same edge as oboe."

I plastered a smile on my face and directed it at the professor, not wanting to speak in case I said the wrong thing again.

He shook his head and raked a hand through his mane of white hair. "It's among the best I've ever heard it played."

He was the most sought-after professor at the school. Influential and powerfully connected, he functioned as a direct conduit to a successful career. Other students had studied with him for years without the kind of praise he expended on me that day. I had been hoping to study with him when I was more advanced, maybe for a graduate degree, but he took a special interest in me after that class. We started weekly lessons in addition to my visits with other teachers, and he started taking me out on weekends to play at events for the Conservatory's richest donors.

It was difficult to make friends after that first studio class. It had been hard already. The youngest person at the Conservatory was fourteen until I showed up at twelve. My new classmates were upset that I was better than them. "Go play your pipa," one of them said to me as I walked out of the hall. I had heard that she was an actual descendant of Franz Joseph Haydn. It was the first time I thought about how strange it was that the thing I spent all my time doing belonged to a culture that wasn't mine. But my parents were the ones who taught me piano. It is just as much a part of my blood as it is hers.

Of all the things said about me during my time there, the whispers about my obsession with death and loneliness didn't bother me much. They weren't too far off. The longer I was away from my parents, the less I was able to remember the feeling of their love, which was buried day after day by the cruel treatment I received from my classmates. Where my peers found and chose to communicate beauty in music, I could find only loss and ugliness. Not the note itself, but the ephemerality, the inability to sustain itself.

My time at the Conservatory was difficult and tumultuous, which might explain why I don't remember it well. Some of the most heartbreaking moments in music happen when composers break a pattern they have established. The contrast between the acceptance I had at home and the hostility I received at school was unbearable, and so I became obsessed with growth and self-improvement.

At first, I wanted more than anything to have friends, to belong. I threw away the food my parents sent me, swallowing the guilt I felt for wasting their money. I started lying to them and keeping most of the stipend money I had planned on giving them. My first winter, I bought extravagant clothing while my parents moved two old electric blankets to whichever surface they were sitting on. They had a small space heater in the piano room for when they taught students. Otherwise, there was not enough money to justify its use. I knew Ma's arthritis was extra painful in the cold, and still, I did not send any money home.

It made me sick to lie to them and I hated myself for it, so I tried to hate them instead. After all, they were the ones who hadn't provided enough for me. But I could still see the look on Ba's face when he took me into his closet the day before I left. His hands shook as he peeled more than half of the paltry bills they had saved over the years, kept in an old shoe box in his dresser, and handed them to me. His generosity had lasted me a month.

I went back to hating myself. I bought the same brands my classmates wore and painted my twelve-year-old face in garish bright colors. I bleached my black hair, which turned orange where it didn't fall out. Looking back, it seems like I had instinctively known that the most effective place to prune myself was at the roots.

A few months into my time at the Conservatory, I was the only student picked to play in a masterclass for a distinguished guest lecturer who had his own highly selective music school in Montreal. I practiced diligently for the masterclass because I was certain there had to be a limit to how much my peers disliked me. There had to exist a level of piano-playing so incredible it would change their minds. I focused on gaining control of sound in new ways. I brought out the piercing anguish of certain harmonies by transforming each finger into the spade tip of a powerful shovel, excavating sound. If the music required something gentler, I could play so softly that the notes almost didn't sound. By the time they reached the audience's ear, they were echoes, made not by my hands but by the hot breath of their coupling. I would transcend, become untouchable, and they would see me for what I could do and not for what I couldn't change about myself.

On the day of the masterclass, I was in the cafeteria studying a music score and spooning tapioca pudding into my mouth when a few older girls walked by. They each had a cup of hot tea, which they tipped onto my hand. Blisters formed immediately. I played in the masterclass anyway, biting my tongue in pain while my right hand oozed pus on the keys.

"What happened to your hand?" Professor Zsaborsky asked.

I lied because I saw how closely my classmates were watching me, daring me to tell on them. The anger and distress had given the piece an emotional expression my professors had hardly thought possible. They all agreed it was my best performance yet. The guest had only positive things to say, and when we were alone backstage, he tried to woo me over to his institution. He insisted on taking me out to a fancy dinner, where he spent most of the time marveling at my ability to play at such a young age a piece that demanded, in his view, the highest understanding of sexual desire. I had played a new and difficult transcription for piano of Astor Piazzolla's *Four Seasons of Buenos Aires*. "You seem to understand that the most powerful thing about lust is not carnal indulgence but restraint. A savage control."

I returned to my room after dinner that night to find all my sheet music torn into fragments and scattered everywhere. I tried for months to reconstruct and tape it together. Eventually I had to concede that the treasured words of musical instruction from my parents were lost. Whoever broke in had also taken the only picture I had, pinned to the wall above my pillow: my parents and me backstage after a competition I had won years ago. The loss of that photo was a turning point. I resolved to stop chasing approval from those who would never give it to me.

The bullying was never that destructive again, but it continued for eight years, the duration of my time at the Conservatory. My relationship with music changed; love became dependency. No matter how dark everything else might have seemed, the music in my mind was a glowing orb. It was my way out of language, out of the societal structures used by others to exclude me. No one could tell from my music how much I did or didn't have, where I was from, or what I looked like. All I wanted to do for the rest of my life was to sit at the piano and urge wood and ivory to speak.

The one good day a year was when my parents came from New Jersey to see me perform in the end-of-year recital. They drove their battered, rusted car, with barely functional seat belts, into the city. It was a big deal for them to cancel their students for even one day. I spent weeks leading up to the recital feeling guilty about the money they would lose because of me. The expression on their faces always made it worthwhile. For the last recital, Ma brought me a dress she had saved for weeks to buy. It was an old-fashioned style, one I wouldn't have picked for myself, but I changed into it right away in one of the school stalls. She was so proud of the dress and how I looked in it.

A girl from my class sauntered past with her impeccably dressed parents and whispered loudly about my dress to her mother: *"Hideous!"*

I smoothed the rough skirt and hugged myself in it, smiling brightly at Ma in case she had understood. Her expression had dimmed. I felt a deep anxiety and shame for myself, and for the pain people casually inflicted on my parents.

At the ticket office, a pimply boy slid a laminated piece of paper toward us. Even with my student discount, the seat prices were too high.

"We sit in back again. Better sound anyway. Look for us, OK?" Ma said. "Anyway, our clothes is not fancy enough."

With my parents in the audience, I always played differently. A professor likened it once to a sort of glow, as if each note had a luminous core that melted into the next and each phrase was a fishing line pulling up strands of flickering iridescent fish.

"You're always a tremendous pianist, but my god, when that quality is present, it's just out of this world. What do you think it is?"

I shrugged modestly, to sidestep the question. The act of transcribing love into another medium was easier to do than to explain. I could almost feel Ma's small quick hands leading mine, phrase by phrase, and I followed the direction of Ba's voice in my head, always singing slightly ahead of what I was playing.

My performance blew away my professors' highest expectations. I could hear Professor Zsaborsky aggressively clapping and cheering over everyone else.

In a way, it was nice to always know where I could find my parents. I would bow at the end of my performance, look up at the back row, and take a picture of them in my mind.

Afterward, they came backstage shyly to congratulate me and to meet with my professors, saying little and understanding less. Ba smiled at everyone, excited to be in an institution dedicated to music again. Ma was happy, too, but she took care to keep her mouth closed. She was always insecure about her teeth because we couldn't afford dental care, and she never wanted to embarrass me with her accented English. Her embarrassment made me sad.

So what if they fumbled their words sometimes? They understood music better than anyone I had ever known, and all I wanted was to make them proud. My classmates and their parents prattled on around us, loudly bragging about their reservations at fancy restaurants in the city with famous chefs and expensive champagne.

"I brought food, we eat together in your room," Ma said.

We went to my little room, and I felt a fresh flood of shame as I saw through their eyes the expensive belongings I had amassed, purchases I had made to fit in with money they needed.

Ma fingered a silk dress in my closet that cost the equivalent of a month of lessons for her.

"So beautiful," she said, holding it against my body. "You deserve most beautiful. Not like one I buy you." She hung it back carefully in the closet, the look on her face making me want to cry.

They unwrapped mushroom-and-chive baozi, potato silk, and winter melon soup. The rice was still steaming. My parents watched as I ate rapidly, quiet for a while.

"We know is hard to be here. But we so proud of you."

The stars outside the window were shining almost as brightly as the city lights when my parents started getting ready to leave. I didn't want them to go. It was too little after so long.

"OK. Thirty more minute. Can't drive too late because teaching tomorrow start very early."

It was the high point of my year. My fingertips had split without Ma's constant care, and each finger looked like a miniature hoof galloping across the piano. That night, I fell asleep to Ma massaging my hands with a large tub of the liniment-supplemented Vaseline she had brought and Ba telling me about his plans for a new piano transcription of one of our favorite folk songs. When I woke up, they were gone. It was early in the morning, but I couldn't sleep after the excitement of the previous night. I went to my practice room, playing until I could see the sun rise through the little window.

Conor Hearst, another of Zsaborsky's students, knocked on my door in the afternoon. He came in out of breath. He had been looking for me everywhere, to tell me about my parents.

CHAPTER FOUR

I am helping Lilith drag long strands of dried kelp from a drawer to throw in the tub.

"Victor runs Organic Provisions now, but he didn't start it. He made a fortune from various tech start-ups, VC, and crypto investments. He was a billionaire before he was twenty-five or something crazy like that.

"His interest in beauty started when his third wife got Botox. The place botched it by giving her too much, and she needed help repairing her face. She called everywhere begging for a miracle no one could deliver until she found Saje, then founder of a small experimental store, who suggested the Chaoshan Mud Treatment.

"Saje rushed her into this exact body pod and filled it with kelp and sake vinegar. The kelp is handpicked from the coast of France and has special salts that denature and tenderize the skin's elastin. The sake vinegar is a rarity aged by monks in Japan for decades to preserve collagen."

"And the crabs? The remora?"

We are lighting candles and placing them on every surface in the room. Next to the tub, we arrange slices of sugared orchids on a gilded tray.

"Saje had the revelation of using remora to siphon toxic elements from people. It's the same general idea as leeches, except they tolerate higher levels of toxicity. The problem is that they excrete the toxicity at a higher rate. That's where the crabs come in. These crabs are a delicacy all over Asia, and on a trip to Chaoshan, Saje learned about their singular capacity for purification. She added them to this treatment, which takes advantage of their remarkable ability to filter nitrates, ammonia, and neurotoxins in general.

"Victor's wife was in this pod for three hours, on a bed of crabs while the remora sucked the cheap shitty Botox out of her skin. Anyway, while Victor's wife was having the procedure done, he and Saje talked, and he tried all kinds of products she had in-store. He was hooked. His wife was the one who went in for the procedure, but they both left transformed."

When we step out to collect him, the immaculate black suit is gone and Victor is wrapped in a luxurious pink robe, fluffy like a giant carnation petal. He turns as we approach, holding a delicate teacup.

"Hi, I'm Victor."

I gasp as he turns to face us.

"Oh, I'm so sorry." He chuckles. "Forgot I had these on. How frightening they must look without context." Victor's face is covered with writhing translucent lavender chunks. He peels one from his cheek and holds it out to me. "Leopard slugs. We've genetically modified them to deep-clean pores enzymatically." He smiles through the purple slime. "It was a collaboration with

Dyson." He looks at it, wriggling in his palm. "Welcome to Holistik. I so look forward to getting to know you more."

He drones for a half hour about leopard slugs and their unique lovemaking before falling asleep. I watch him more closely while he is slumbering, trying to remember where I've seen him before. He is an attractive man, undeniably so, but there is something unnatural about his face. Even without the slugs, his face is doughy as if new skin has been grafted on unsuccessfully, sitting on top of his face like gobs of damp flesh. It reminds me of something I saw long ago, a street vendor straining fresh tofu curds.

CHAPTER FIVE

You're working where?" Alice asks as I trudge through the door with bags and bags from Holistik.

"Let me help you put everything away," she says, practically tearing the iconic silk sacks out of my hands and ripping them open to see the items inside.

Her face is red, and she tells me she's exhausted from exorcising the spleen of a Nazi from a futon in Tribeca. For the first time, I think that my workday could actually compare with hers in novelty. My space in the fridge is suddenly filled with juices, broths, and tonics. The pantry is stuffed with dusts, flakes, and pills. Our bookshelf is transformed into a sculpture garden of beauty devices. She helps me drag everything else down the stairs to my basement apartment. Next to the soiled air mattress and the dirty concrete floor, the satiny bags look absurd.

How to describe my roommates? Charlie Hess and Alice Blanton met each other while they were both in other relationships.

"But we just knew," Alice told me the first time I met them, her long glittery nails digging into Charlie's arm.

On the phone, I had noticed Alice's voice was pitched impressively high, a sort of constant baby voice with sprinkles of laughter that made me curious about the evolutionary distance between humans and dolphins. She laughs so incessantly, she often has to gasp in the middle of her giggling before she can continue.

Charlie, on the other hand, rarely speaks. Between his total lack of verbosity and her constant barrage of noise, it's debatable who says the least.

When they interviewed me to be their roommate, they didn't tell me I would be living in, essentially, a cave.

"Only $1,100!" the girl had said sweetly on the phone. "For so much square footage. It's basically a brownstone, you know, like *Sex and the City*? You don't? Well, anyway, it's awesome and that price is, like, unheard of in New York. Where are you from?"

"What do you mean?" I asked, taken aback by the abrupt question.

"You haven't heard of *Sex and the City*, so I'm assuming you're not from here."

"I'm from New Jersey," I said truthfully.

She was silent until I finally relented.

"My parents are from China, though."

"Amazing. I love Pocky. Is that Chinese? And sushi, of course. Or wait, that's Japanese? I'm terrible. So excited to learn about authentic Asian food and culture from you!"

"Are there windows?" I asked, to change the subject.

"Yes, of course!" Alice said.

I should have been more specific. There are windows on the first floor that extend to the top of my basement-level wall. I can't even reach the bottom ledge on tiptoe. When I found a chair on the street in my first few weeks and carried it home, I used it to hoist myself up to clean the furred grime from the glass. When I was done, I had a remarkably clear view of the dark soil into which the building was sinking.

Like a lot of girls at the Conservatory, Alice is a perfectionist, especially regarding her appearance. She refuses food so often and so virtuously, I would believe her if she told me she's on a subscription service that miraculously places everything she doesn't eat into someone else's starving belly.

Only when I started living with Alice did I realize how many of my former classmates had kept such thin bodies. Maybe I hadn't been better at the piano than the other girls but simply less hungry. If they had nourished their bodies, their fingertips might have filled out and their sound on the piano could have projected farther. It would have been a gamble. In the classical music field, it's still more permissible for women to be mediocre than it is for them to be fat.

Alice is trying to make it as a feng shui practitioner specializing in exorcising intergenerational trauma from furniture. I'm not sure what "making it" would mean in her chosen field. Artistic director of exorcism at *Architectural Digest*? Head undead curator at the Met? Every couple of days, she comes home with a new piece of furniture, circling it for minutes with narrowed eyes.

"It's just weeping and weeping," she said once, shaking her head at an ornate high-back chair.

Charlie has a fairly high-paying job in tech security and a profitable hobby of buying and reselling sneakers, clothing, and streetwear accessories. Between the two of them, they appropriate an impressive number of cultures.

For the last decade of my life, I had practiced eight to ten hours a day. But now that I am without a piano, I have no idea how to spend my time. My life, which had been so predictable before, was now stuck in that blank space between keys, treading silence.

Before I found work at the restaurant, I mostly read want ads, took long walks on the weekends in Brooklyn Bridge Park, applied unsuccessfully to jobs, and tried to pretend my depression was the same thing as Alice and Charlie's favorite activity, lounging. Even the way they say the word *lounging* drips with lazy pleasure.

"It's Sunday, I just want to lounge," Alice would say sleepily, moving to the couch as if through molasses.

They are prodigies of indolence, unparalleled in the number of ways they have conceived of sitting on a couch. They charge me over $1,000 a month for my shallow basement grave and sleep like babies above me in CBD-emitting snooze pods while I wake every morning with pruned fingertips and dirt inexplicably under my fingernails. Still, being a classical musician has prepared me for a life surrounded by wealth I can't access, and I can't help noting the space is just big enough for a piano if I can ever afford one.

The smell of mildew emanates from the air mattress where I sit looking into a cracked full-length mirror. I can hear Alice and Charlie upstairs.

"How did she get a job there?"

"Babe."

"It's not fair!"

"Babe."

Her envy helps a little with the realization that I have no one to tell about my new job.

"She's so lucky!"

I try that luck in the bathroom, but the showerhead, covered in something mysterious and granular, refuses to do more than leak a few drops.

I put some clothes on and take out my phone. Matchmaker, matchmaker, make me a match. Preferably one with steady hot water and a clean fluffy towel I can poach.

CHAPTER SIX

stare up at a massive town house.

The door clicks open and swings back violently from the wind.

"Jesus, it's cold!" Henry, twenty-nine, looks me up and down with suspicion. Surprisingly, he looks exactly like the photos he uses online, the ones that depict him as a tall and generically handsome blond.

"Did you knock?"

"I was about to."

"I fell asleep. Thought I'd missed you." He lets me in.

"This is where you live?" I look around with ill-concealed awe, suddenly self-conscious about how I look, how I must smell.

He rubs his eyes tiredly. "Yeah."

I sleep with strangers often, but none have granted me access to a place, let alone a neighborhood, as nice as this one. Henry was a bit farther than I would have liked to travel, but he dressed in photos (when he was dressed at all) exceptionally well and was so far the only person to click the *must-have!* button for me instead of just *add to cart!*

Sometimes it feels like the whole city is swiping furiously on

devices. I once watched an entire subway platform of people con-
ducting a silent orchestral piece on their phones with the same
repeated gestures. I use the old press kit photos I have from the
Conservatory of me standing in front of a piano. Who can turn
down professional pictures of a young Asian woman who is probably good with her hands?

There had been a clumsy few at the Conservatory. In such a
competitive setting, it was difficult to do anything without the
entire school finding out within a day. The students and teachers
monitored each other's every movement with a frenzy.

The few who slept with me never told anyone because they
were afraid of being ridiculed. There was only one boy, Conor
Hearst, who was found out because he was a repeat offender. The
first time, he was so drunk, it was justifiable. The second and
third times, however, he was sober. The last time it happened, he
was getting ready to go in the half-dark and taking so much time
I stupidly wondered if he was stalling because he had feelings
for me.

It happened enough in the movies I watched. The most popular guy in school would fall in love with the ugly unpopular girl,
and his desire would instantly make her worthy in the eyes of
everyone else.

Every movie I watched alone at night repeated itself in a simu-
lacrum of this plotline. After Conor expressed a drunken sexual
interest in me that first time, I became cautiously optimistic
about the possibility of this narrative happening in my own life.

I didn't have anything to lose by asking him if he had feelings
for me, so I did.

He looked at me thoughtfully for a few minutes. His light

blue eyes were silvery in the dim light, and his lashes curled upward like the tendrils of hope rising in my chest.

"You're a really good pianist," he said softly before sliding off my bed and padding away in his mismatched socks.

I lay back in a puddle of moonlight, melting at the first positive words from a classmate in years. A few weeks later I heard he was back with a girlfriend I hadn't known he had.

Up a flight of stairs to the first room on the right. Henry shuts the door and pounces on me, undressing me quickly. Within a few minutes, he is inside me, thrusting and grunting occasionally. His breathing hardens and his eyes go blank, concentrating on something ahead of him.

Like the others, he is an unremarkable fuck, perfunctorily performing missionary for not too long or short a time. In a way, it's his perfect averageness that gets me excited.

I settle in and imagine the bathroom I am about to use. What kind of showerhead will this place have? What scent will the soap be? Rose, I think. Not the cheap candied rose scent in Alice's products, but real rose scent, from essential oils or England. He gasps and then covers my abdomen thickly before hopping off and grabbing a tissue box. He hands me two of them, and I dab my stomach.

"Would you mind if I used your shower really quickly? The super hasn't fixed my drain in, like, days."

"It's down the hallway on the right," he mumbles, already half asleep.

I walk down a wide hallway with smooth wood planks,

enjoying the realization that none of Alice's negative-calorie granola (it takes more energy to shit it out!) or her cat's organic kitty litter will stab my feet. I turn into the first doorway on the right and feel for a switch. Light pink marble swirls all around me, and the black and white floor tiles look like enormous piano keys.

"Hi."

A curly blond head floats in a soaking tub filled with bubbles. A pair of immense grayish-blue eyes looks at me curiously.

"I'm so sorry. I didn't know anyone was in here." I am horrified.

"It's OK. I should get out anyway. I always fall asleep and come out a raisin." She holds out a wrinkled hand for me to see.

The head rising from the water is connected to a body covered in creamy white foam. She steps gingerly over the side of the tub onto a plush bathmat. I watch as she lifts her arms, gently gathering her long thick hair above her head, breasts jiggling delicately with the motion.

"Who are you?"

"I'm here with—" I don't remember his name.

"Henry?"

"Yes. Henry."

"I'm Helen. His twin." She walks over to me still covered in a lace of suds and sticks out her hand. Bubbles crackle like electricity as they pop against my skin.

"Are you taking a shower? Here, let me set it up for you. It's a little complicated the first time." She leans into the shower and messes around with the dials. I clutch the shredded tissue stuck to my stomach, hoping she hasn't noticed it. The water comes on, washing the remaining foam from her body.

I force myself to look away as she straightens herself.

"There you go." She laughs at my expression. "No need to be embarrassed. It was very nice to meet you."

I close the door behind her and lock it. My face, reflected in the mirror, is bright red.

Like her brother, she is also blond and blue-eyed, but she is maybe the least average person I have ever seen. From inside the shower, I notice she hasn't drained the bathtub. Steam rises furiously from the water, and strands of her light honey hair lie on the lip of the tub like chains of exquisite gold.

CHAPTER SEVEN

t's four in the morning when I get home. I love slipping back
into the city after a stolen hot shower, maybe grabbing a stale
bagel and some lukewarm coffee as I sync my legs to the crowds
of people walking purposefully toward a new day. I check the
living room for one of Charlie's many laptops and locate one
under a couch cushion. Thankfully, Alice has too many trust issues for Charlie's devices to have a password. I consider logging
in to one of Charlie's social media accounts. I long ago gave up
on my own, embarrassed by the number of accounts I followed
and how few followed me back. But if I logged in, what would I
search for? I regret not getting Henry's last name, one he unques-
tionably shares with his sister. I open a private tab.

First, I decide to look up Lilith, to see what I can find about
her and her estranged director father. At the film center across
from the Conservatory, I watched his films, usually set in Hong
Kong and China. They made me feel closer to my parents and
led to hours spent dreaming of a place, a life, where I fit in
naturally.

The only mention I find of Lilith's name is from years ago, for a journalism student at a private women's college. Besides dark hair, she bears very little resemblance to the woman I met yesterday. I click on her father's last name instead and search his features for similarities. The same pearlescent skin and slightly upturned eyes. I feel a stab of resentment before reason kicks in. I work to rid myself of the envy I so often felt in grade school and at the Conservatory for those who are half Asian, reminding myself that it doesn't necessarily guarantee more assimilation.

There are countless profiles of Victor. Variations of the same rags-to-riches story. He grew up impoverished with an absent father and a constantly pregnant mother, and his life was hell until he clawed his way to Caltech, where he revolutionized the suturing technology being used in hospitals. He expanded into a myriad of other sectors and invested in different start-ups before giving Saje the capital to start Organic Provisions when he was only twenty-eight.

He was so adept at investing that the nootropic supplement truBrain, which promises better financial decision-making, was developed using his brain scans. Today he is one of the richest men in the world and he uses his money to make the world a more beautiful place. He owns land to protect and preserve it. Builds museums for the art he collects. Gives generously to music and arts foundations. Owns countless companies responsible for the research and development of new medical technologies and equipment. I have a vision of him as an octopus with an inky indelible limb in every field. He even single-handedly funded the Conservatory concert hall I practically grew up performing in.

There are scientific papers denouncing or exalting the procedures and ingredients used at Holistik. Allegations of fearmongering as a marketing scheme. Celebrities are split between those who use their influence to warn people about the dangers of Holistik, and others who fly in on private jets to get their favorite facials and body treatments and to cuddle with the animals at the Zoo.

I fast-forward through a mini documentary about the Zoo, Organic Provisions' collection of animals being humanely raised and researched for science and skin care purposes.

I take a virtual tour of the Organic Provisions farm a couple of hours from the city in the Shawangunk Mountains. The farmers are all beautiful men and women, frozen on-screen with light blond hair, their minimal clothing flecked with rose gold and terra-cotta clay.

I skip through a promotional video of Sloane, a top-tier nose and the head of fragrance at Holistik, picking fresh lavender and distilling it for the company's signature perfume. There must be hundreds of hours of video tutorials on Holistik products, including ones from a former employee teasing a forthcoming tell-all.

There are dissertations on farming techniques written in Hungarian and Japanese, photos of Victor with pop stars, famous chefs, and heads of state, and at G8 summits. Right-wing blogs speculate that the company is a sex cult, that it grows illegal substances or, worse, harbors illegal immigrants. A podcast series details recently dropped claims that the farm is on sacred Native American burial grounds.

With zero evidence and for no apparent reason, a group of people on the internet fervently believe Victor to be a descendant of the Vanir, a group of deities in Norse mythology. An old photo of him on the website with two blond children (labeled a niece and nephew) ignites a heated debate in tacky pseudo-runic type-faces about whether these twins could be reincarnations of Freyja and Freyr.

There is an unceasing amount of scandalous lawsuits, most of them by ex-wives who claim Victor pursued legal ownership of their bodies while they were married. His first wife died a few years ago in a tragic car accident, and he had controversially destroyed a small forest of ancient trees for their unique resin to preserve and encase her in amber.

I bookmark pages and open tabs to read as I go, but there doesn't seem to be an end to the amount of information available about Victor. It's as if people are actively writing and uploading more and more opinions, conjectures, and hearsay. I stop knowing what, if anything, I can believe.

I finally resurface when I hear Alice from the room next door, yawning loudly before the incessant pinging of her phone starts.

CHAPTER EIGHT

The first thing they teach me at the store is how to be my best self. It requires constant self-surveillance to steadily improve. My coworkers relate it to pruning a bonsai. Painful but necessary for refinement. What starts as an enthusiasm for improvement becomes an all-consuming infatuation. Caution becomes paranoia and, eventually, fear. Is there anything more comforting in life than knowing what to fear? At Holistik, they teach me what I need to be afraid of to become beautiful.

I learn what not to eat (almost everything). What not to drink (almost everything). But science changes quickly, and often. Don't eat eggs. Eat three eggs a day before five p.m. Only drink the albumen of the egg, and only at dawn, by the sea. Eventually there are places and substances to avoid. Specific energies are not allowed, and certain feelings are cautioned against. The compendium of things to fear is so vast, it often feels too risky to take a deep breath.

It is an exhilarating place to work. Fast-paced and rewarding. Our clientele comes from all over the world: rich individuals who desperately want to improve themselves. We charge a steep price for our terrifying knowledge, but those who can afford it are rewarded with the most exceptional beauty.

People are more interested in me when they discover I work at Holistik. They display a slight but unmistakable deference, a hint of envy I surprise myself by enjoying. I first notice it with Alice, who starts saving me coffee in the mornings and offering me a seat on her beloved couch whenever I am home. Men, in particular, treat me differently. They offer to walk me home, give me drinks "on the house," their desire evidently inspiring kindness.

When I left the sheltered Conservatory, New York City had felt unstable. Like I was standing on shifting sands without hope of finding purchase or purpose. I watched as everyone around me enjoyed this aspect of the city, which, in its infinite sea of change, always offered something new to eat, fuck, or be.

Now I sprinkle the name Holistik into more of my interactions to enjoy the subtle benefits of its fame. Even my walk has changed. As if my body is mechanized by an inexorable pull toward anything I want. In the store with my gray silk Holistik sheath concealing cheap polyester underwear, I feel the compulsion and power of beauty, the way necks bend everywhere I go. At last, the land of opportunity has stretched an exclusive hand toward me. Is this how my parents felt, landing on the tarmac of a new and unfamiliar country, trying to twist their tongues in a new language? Afraid and lonely, yet powerful?

Even though the pay is better than any of the restaurant jobs I had before, my financial situation remains precarious. No matter how hard I try to save, it's almost impossible not to hemorrhage money in New York. I remember my parents holding my hand up to the light when I was small, remarking on the lack of gaps between my fingers when I squeezed them together.

"No money escape your hands," they exclaimed proudly. How I wish that were the case. Still, I try my best, working every day of the week for eight, sometimes nine, hours. I enjoy being alone at the store in the mornings, so I leave home early to arrive before my shift. It reminds me of the Conservatory, where I would sit at the piano, playing the score of the sunrise. I do a sweep as I enter, opening testers and making sure the products are fully stocked on the floor. Then I make my way downstairs to brew drinks for the day's spa guests. It is a pleasure to mix the herbal powders and to sprinkle them into beautiful white vessels to steep. When the opening tasks are taken care of, I sit on a meditation cloud by myself with a book, enjoying the silence and space, the rarity of not having anyone else's feelings to consider except my own.

The other girls straggle in eventually, and once we are all present, Imogen, our spiritual nutritionist and the chief wellness officer of Holistik, virtually conducts us in an aura weigh-in and gratitude blessing. We each get a spritz on our wrists of estratetraenol and ambergris to make ourselves primally irresistible to our customers. Lilith then gives us our tasks and goals for the day, and we go upstairs to wait for our clients.

I try my best to be a model employee—to work my way to belonging. I replay every interaction with my coworkers and customers, trying to make sure I didn't fuck up in any way. I feel an intense pressure to be perfect in order to show my gratitude. I have a difficult time comprehending how I have come to be in this rarified position and worry that any misstep will result in my dismissal.

I am vigilant about swapping testers and cleaning out the trash cans. I replenish the inventory every hour and take short lunch breaks, unlike the other girls, who might languish downstairs divining their green juice remnants for hours. I am used to the rigorous schedule necessary for piano and realize my body has missed repetitive labor. Saje brags about me to the other girls.

"You know me, I would never go to a restaurant that doesn't readily cater to the temple diet! And yet, right after my personal session with Immy, I had the most intense craving. I thought I was going fermental! I even had fries! Don't worry, I had a celery enema the next day. Anyway, when I saw this one, I knew it was kismet. That's why you should always listen to your body."

Many of the customers assume I have knowledge about our products from Asia, and some speak very slowly, afraid I might not understand English. I never correct them, and with enough studying, I do eventually become an expert in Korean skin care products and traditional Chinese medicinal remedies. My favorite thing to do at the store is to give makeovers using our products. Zsaborsky had always maintained that there are no bad pieces of music; the fault of an unsuccessful performance is that of the performer. I start to feel similarly about faces. Music and makeup are both about attention direction. In both, you have to know which features and phrases to conceal or amplify. In the first couple of weeks, I am too friendly when I am doing makeovers.

Lilith reprimands me. "We aren't selling products. We're selling a lifestyle. Desire. The possibility for them to become us."

From then on, I am still always exceptionally polite, but cool in the Holistik way, making sure they know I am part of an *us* that they are not.

We are often subjected to long conversations with our customers to make a sale. They waltz in wanting their regular girl so they can catch her up on every inane thing their spouse has said since their last spending spree at Holistik.

Clients waiting in line justify their purchases by murmuring the word *self-care* as they hold their new products as tightly as a nun might grasp her rosary. I first heard this magical word from a woman who came in with her daughter, a rare teenager completely unimpressed with Holistik.

"Everyone who works here looks the same. It's creepy," she said before accidentally stepping on my foot.

I had also noticed a pattern in the coloring and features of my coworkers but know it's a result of their competitiveness. Emerson will make a little tweak to her supplements or get a new procedure done, and Madison will follow or get a quickie at the nearest Holistik-sanctioned Botox drive-thru until all the girls look more or less the same again. Why work in an environment that offers endless upgrades for desirability if not to take advantage?

The daughter points at Cassandrea and then at Tanner. "I mean, are they twins? Seriously, everyone looks exactly the same!"

"Well, not everyone," the mother said, looking at me kindly.

I was stuck with them for almost two hours. The mother was intent on lecturing me and her daughter about self-care and its incompatibility with the male gaze.

"Society wants us to look for the approval of men in everything we do. Self-care is the radical act of dressing and living for ourselves."

The male gaze is a new concept for me. It had never occurred to me to dress for men. I have only ever hoped to get the approval and acceptance of other women, specifically those who don't even think of me as someone worthy of exclusion.

When I get home at night, I spend two to three hours doing my prescribed facial and body care routines. I prop my phone against the stack of free books I've accumulated from the city sidewalks and watch the shows my parents and I used to watch as I cleanse, tone, and massage. Through the cracked screen, people in buildings barge in on one another, create and resolve conflicts, and fall in love while I exfoliate, microcurrent, and mask. Sometimes, the laugh tracks make me feel like my parents are with me. Other times, they make me feel more alone.

Victor rarely comes to the store in a work capacity, but we see him often for various treatments and procedures. The other girls are skittish in front of him, nervously blabbing about their boyfriends or their fathers, all of whom would love an endorsement from him at this investment securities firm or that new fintech start-up. He appears to listen intently, concentrating on them with extreme focus. It's envy-inducing, as if nothing else exists for him in that moment.

"Go on," he says generously to the girls, continuing to feign interest while making adjustments, adding, subtracting, whittling, and decoloring until he has a perfect picture of them in his head. A few hours or a day later, Saje will discreetly suggest new supplements or surgeries for the girl to try. Except for Cassandrea, who told Victor her boyfriend could use a good word at one of his companies because she was pregnant, and they needed more income to support the coming baby. The next day, Saje offered Cassandrea prenatal maternity leave.

Not all of the work at Holistik is glamorous. Because I am usually the first to get to the store, I'm often tasked with the job of warding off the homeless people who sleep overnight in the Holistik doorway. The other girls wouldn't do it anyway, having made it clear that they believe homelessness to be a contagious spiritual or moral failure. I was just getting started on the daily tasks one morning when Saje rushed down to find me. She explained that she had stepped over a body to get in the store and that I needed to deal with it immediately. "I would do it, but my contentment level would drop too low for me to consider an altercation this early in the morning. You're so much stronger than I am. So resilient!"

I hadn't seen anyone on my way in, so I looked out of the front window to confirm that there was someone in the doorway. I couldn't see anyone. I opened the door a crack and saw a frail Asian man bundled in rags, huddled in a corner. My heart hurt to see that he was around the same age as Ba. He shouldn't have been out in the cold like this, with dirty clothes and a collection of waste surrounding him. We didn't encounter as many homeless people in New Jersey, but my parents always gave the coins they had. It was only narrowly that they had escaped that life themselves. From the corner of my eye, I could see Saje's red hair. She was watching me. I shook the man's shoulder, as gently as I could. He opened a bruised eye and looked at me with a desperation I had never seen before.

"Five more minute," he said softly, like a child bartering with his mother.

"I'm so sorry," I whispered. "You have to leave."

"Please," he said through numb lips.

Saje was still watching. I tentatively grabbed his bare arm. His eyes flew open at that moment and looked down at my hand violating his space and body. Saje had moved closer to the window, the red of her hair a sign to discontinue feelings of empathy. I watched as my arm strengthened its grip on his, yanking him roughly to his feet.

"You have to leave! You can't sleep here!" I said to him. I said other things, too, screamed them. I started crying, hearing the things I was saying. My vision blurred with tears, and he looked even more like Ba. I wondered what my parents would think if they saw me in this moment. He left in a hurry when my ranting became crying, looking back at me once in disbelief. I wiped the spittle from my mouth and went back inside the store. For the rest of the day, I kept seeing the look he gave me, like I was a wild animal.

CHAPTER NINE

My heart drops into the pit of my stomach when I see Margot. I am perpetually a couple of months behind on rent, and my inbox is drowning with unopened emails from Applebaum. She comes out from behind the desk and pulls me aside.

"You know I want to, but I can't cover you for much longer. They're already asking questions, and soon I won't be able to hold them off."

I tell her about the new job, how well it pays, and she softens, seeming genuinely happy for me.

"How are they today?"

"OK. Same old."

We walk together to the elevator and ride up to the third floor.

"Guess who's here!"

I appreciate that Margot puts on a chipper voice for them, even though they rarely respond. She opens the frayed curtain separating their beds from one another.

"You OK in here?"

I nod. "I won't be long. I just want to tell them about the new job."

"OK. I'll be back in fifteen."

I wait until her orthopedic squelches reach the far end of the hallway, and then I speak to my parents.

"Hi, Ma. Ba."

I love them so much in these moments when I first see them, before that love is replaced by a terrible yearning for the people they used to be. I walk between them and take a hand from each. They are surprisingly warm.

"I'm sorry I haven't visited as much the last couple weeks. I got a new job, and I was busy with the training for it. I'll have more time to visit now. And I can make sure you stay here."

I look around at the only accommodation I can afford to secure for them and want to cry. They deserve so much better. Real beds instead of rickety cots. Fresh flowers instead of plastic potted pants.

"You would love it, Ma. I wish I could take you." I think of all the times she would come backstage before a competition or a concert to put a bit of her lipstick on my mouth with a finger. "You don't need," she would say, "but just for fun." Now I take a tube of Holistik's dahlia blossom lipstick from my bag and lightly spread a thin layer over her cracked lips. The contrast between her bloodless face and the vivid pink lipstick is unsettling. I wipe it off gently.

I remember when she would come home with a new perfume sample she had gotten from a store, how she would dab it on the same places on our bodies. Even though they had so little money,

my parents always managed to provide me with not only neces-
sities but even luxuries. It hurts that I am failing them now when
they need me.

I wait to see if either of them will respond. Ba's mouth falls
open once before closing again. Ma's hand twitches a little in
mine as I try to massage it the way she always massaged my hands
after piano practice. I stroke her arm where the metal crushed it,
almost thankful she isn't conscious enough to process what happened to her hands in the accident.

"I love you both."

I kiss them each on the forehead and leave. Sometimes I have
the energy to talk and talk, but today I duck into the bathroom
and allow myself to cry for a bit before composing myself. It is
hard to see their shrinking frames and shredded lips. In the
stained bathroom mirror, I watch as tears fall from Ma's eyes onto
Ba's nose. It gives me some comfort, at least, to see their features
preserved in me.

There is so much I want to ask them. Everything I want to
know, I ask myself as them. But I don't have the imagination to
invent their history and lack the particulars of their memory.
Every answer ends up taking me further away from the truth of
who they are.

By the time Margot comes back for me, I am standing outside
my parents' room, looking as if I have just left. I want to com-
plain to her about the pungent urine smell; they aren't being
changed often enough, and their skin is so dry—are they getting
enough water? But I can hardly make demands with the amount
of money I owe. As I leave, relief floods my body, followed quickly
by shame. Seeing them is always more difficult than I want to

admit. I had always assumed love carried itself easily through various permutations and disintegrations. Now I find myself disassociating them from the people I had known my parents to be.

I can't decide which is worse, coming up against the limitations of their souls or the limitations of my love.

CHAPTER TEN

walk into Holistik with a cup of coffee and a plain bagel, wary of being judged by the other girls. Caffeine and carbohydrates are both toxins, as far as my peers are concerned. My coworkers are what Imogen calls "self-motivated" because they're always on different experimental diets for their skin or spiritual health. Tanner is only eating an ounce of raw meat a day, and Emerson fasts for three days a week, drinking only peony-and-licorice tea on those days. Madison practices a religion called Dianaism. When she first told me about it, I assumed it was something I hadn't heard of because it was too elevated for me. Over the course of many months, I learned that Dianaism is the worship and ardent endeavor to eat, dress, and live like Princess Diana.

I stop walking just inside the door. Instead of the usual meditative music of female monks chanting and plucking the lyre by running water, something else is playing. Something familiar. My eyes are drawn to the back of the store, where the sun is catching on a slow drip of honey hair. It's the twin from a few weeks ago, Helen. She is chewing on a long stalk of her hair, standing on one leg with the other tucked up like a heron. My coworkers are clustered around her, absorbed in something she is showing them. Does she know them? Customers are also gawking at her coltish beauty. They linger nearby, pretending to look at products.

The sweet down on her arms shines like pale fire in the light, and her large white hands look like blue-veined marble boiled into a soft cream and poured. I look down at my own hands, still recovering from their dishwashing days. Helen is holding one of the tablets used by the store to serve customers. Everyone is watching something on it together. Lilith looks extra sweet resting a cheek on Helen's shoulder in a light blue dress with a dainty ruffled collar. They must know each other, somehow. I am wondering what could be holding everyone in rapture when I hear myself.

My graduation recital, the Rachmaninoff at record-breaking speed. The last time my parents heard me. Panic rises in my body. If I keep playing, the rest of the night will unspool in the same sickening way. I ball up my fists and tighten them until pain shoots through my arm and I feel myself crumpling.

My eyes adjust slowly, assembling Helen piece by piece. A concerned blue eye, a hand wrapping firmly around my waist, soft ringlets pillowing my head as she helps me up and practically carries me downstairs.

She deposits me on a meditation couch and places a hand on either side of my face.

"Are you OK?" she asks.

"Yes, sorry. I don't know what came over me."

"Don't apologize. That was quite the fall. Let's take a few deep breaths together, OK?"

I nod.

I follow her long inhales, watching as her chest swells, and exhale slowly, conscious of our breaths mingling between us. Her hands lower, and she rubs my neck, my temples, behind my ears.

"Thank you," I murmur with closed eyes.

"I'll be right back," she whispers.

She walks to the kitchen and comes back with a washcloth and a little bowl topped with floating petals.

"Crushed violets and calendula flowers." She dips the cloth and gently dabs at my forehead.

I close my eyes again, enjoying the exquisite coolness.

"I've been a bit clumsy lately, and this tincture helps me with the headaches after a fall."

I open my eyes when she starts wiping my arms.

"You spilled your coffee."

I glance down at my sleeves, now dip-dyed dark brown.

"Hey, I feel like that was my fault, and I'm sorry about the video. It clearly made you uncomfortable. You weren't around and I wanted to show Lilith, but then it went on the store speakers, and everyone kind of crowded around."

"That's OK." So I'm not losing my mind. How did she know about my graduation recital? Had she somehow found my name and looked me up online?

Her eyes suddenly widen with alarm. "I just realized that you must be so confused! I'm not stalking you or anything, I promise. I did ask Henry for your name that night, just to confirm you were who I thought you were, but I'm here to drop off ceramics. I make the jars for the products . . . and Victor is my uncle."

I don't know how to respond. I open my mouth anyway, but thankfully she interrupts me.

"This is going to sound super creepy, but I grew up watching you! I think your dad was posting videos of your practice sessions online? My parents made me take piano lessons and I was terrible, but I loved watching you play. Victor even took me to see your concerts at the Conservatory. I'm sure you hear this all the time, but you were a huge inspiration. I never got as good as you, of course, but I've loved music ever since. Thanks to you."

My cheeks are flushing dangerously.

"Are you still playing?"

I hesitate, almost wishing I could say yes, just to make her happy.

"Not really," I say instead.

She looks genuinely afflicted by my answer. "Why not?"

"It's a long story."

Her eyes consider mine. "I happen to love long stories. Are you busy tomorrow night? We could have dinner?"

I stop breathing, afraid that if anything in the atmosphere shifts, she'll change her mind. Saje is calling for me from upstairs. How long has she been repeating my name?

"Yeah, sure. Dinner."

Her face breaks into a bright smile, and I consider shielding my eyes. "Wonderful. I'll cook, it'll be my treat."

I find it difficult to leave her presence. When I finally wrench myself away, every consecutive step is harder to take.

Upstairs, Saje assesses me with concern.

"Is everything all right?"

"Oh, yes. I was just surprised by the music," I say.

She looks confused.

"That's why I fell earlier. I'm fine, though," I tell her hastily.

"You fell? How awful. I'm referring to your stats. It looks as if it's been a highly emotional day for you."

"My stats?" Now it's my turn to be confused.

"From your mandala, darling." She puts a finger to the pebble resting in the soft hollow of my neck. "Did you have an emotional day?"

I look at her, startled. I hadn't realized the necklace was anything besides an aesthetically pleasing alarm clock for my supplements.

"I guess I did," I say frankly, thinking of my parents.

"I am so sorry to hear that, dear. It seems quite traumatic. The important thing is not to blame yourself. We all have our days. That's why we have the mandalas, so our growth is measurable and improvable. Why don't you take your lunch break now? A half hour with Immy will perk you right up."

Imogen's office is in the spa wing. She doesn't like to meet with us in a group, or even individually, because our auras can too easily overtake her energy, causing an imbalance.

"I've worked tirelessly to make my aura as empathic as possible, which makes me powerful but also vulnerable," she explained to me in our first session. "It's worth it, though, because I get to work with you all."

She opens the door and rushes me in.

"You poor thing," she murmurs.

She gestures for me to sit in the chair across from her desk. As soon as I sit, the dark red leather, soft and pliant, starts to move over my limbs, curling like a tongue around my arms, my legs, and the top of my head. A slight vibration begins, and I find myself relaxing. Occasionally, Imogen glances at me, but most of the time, her eyes stay glued to a screen where numbers flash and jump.

I close my eyes and give myself over to the gentle thrum coursing through my body. My heart quickens when I realize another flap of leather has sprung up between my thighs, darting there rapidly. My breathing becomes shallow, and I open my eyes. Imogen is gazing at me encouragingly.

Suddenly, the vibrating stops. Imogen gets up from her chair.

"I'm so sorry about this, it's been malfunctioning all week."

She drags a chair next to me and puts four fingers to my groin. My body reacts immediately, but I'm tightly strapped to the chair, unable to snap my legs together. She looks at me with sympathy.

"It's not ideal for me to do this manually either, but we can't have you being sad for the rest of the day. It's not healthy for you to live with emotional pain, especially since our customers can pick up on it." She starts moving her hand in circles with her eyes locked on the computer screen. "Come on, come on," she mutters to herself.

I realize that until I finish, I won't be allowed to leave. I close my eyes and try to pretend her hand is mine, though her touch is rough and overwhelming. I cycle through images in my mind, landing on one from a few weeks ago of a glistening body rising from a bathtub and covered in foam.

Imogen cheers and I open my eyes. The red chair releases me from its grasp, and I stand up, my legs shaking a bit from the experience. She squirts her hands with sanitizer before opening the door.

"All better?" she asks.

I hesitate, but before I can say anything, she has returned to her desk and clicked through my stats.

"All better," she proclaims, hopping up to shut the door on me.

I walk out of the spa wing and back into the store. On the floor, customers are being taken around by Madison and Emerson. Tanner is restocking products. It's all so normal, making me wonder if I imagined everything. Helen is still here, talking with Saje and Lilith. My cheeks burn at the sight of her, thinking about what just happened. Which was what, exactly? Helen's shadow stretches back to where I am standing. I have to stop myself from lightly tracing the edge of it with my foot. Something she says ignites peals of laughter from the people who have flocked around her. She hugs my coworkers, shoulders a light linen tote, and walks out of Holistik. Time resumes as soon as she is out of sight.

"Feeling better?" Saje has appeared at my side. "That was your first time in the chair, right?"

I nod.

"Amazing, isn't it? We found out through years of research that women who work hard are often unable to make time for pleasure. Since we employ mostly females, we wanted to build in ways of ensuring they can have it all."

"Earlier you said . . . about the mandalas. They take my stats?" I ask.

"Yes. It's based on the same tachistoscope technology we have in-store."

"What is a tachistoscope?" I struggle to repeat the word.

"It's a technology that tracks eye movement, pupil dilation, even how long your eye settles on a product or part of a product. The mandalas infer emotional content from your autonomic nervous system responses."

"That exists?" If what she's saying is true, private moments, vices, and indulgences don't exist.

She rolls her eyes as if my reaction is adorably quaint. "I guarantee it's already being used by every app on your phone. We're one of the first to implement it physically in a store because Victor owns one of the best tachistoscope companies, RealSight."

"It doesn't sound real."

"I know. It's brilliant. Mainly, we use it to learn how to grab and maintain the attention of consumers. We want to learn how to better serve our customers. The more we learn, the more we can anticipate their desires. Technology is the biggest blessing in that way. Good or bad, we all want to be absolved of our choices.

"Of course, we use it to serve our employee family as well. After all, we care about each and every one of you. It's better for business, too. Can't sell wellness if you aren't well."

"Right. And where does this information go?"

"Don't worry. Imogen, Victor, and I are the only ones with access to this information."

I rarely have plans after work, so I go on long walks by myself. I like to be out when the sky dims and the streetlamps turn on. I can look in at the happy families sitting down to dinner together.

This city is so expensive, and yet there seem to be so many who manage to live with comfort, even excess. Today I think about stopping in a historic bookstore on West 10th Street or going into the small tea shop I know some of my coworkers frequent, but I don't dare dream of spending money on anything besides rent for myself or my parents. Rotting pumpkins left over from Halloween a month ago loiter in front of stores. On Christopher Street, in a store window lined with crystals, a woman stirs a big black cauldron with one hand while scrolling her phone with the other. I wonder if the crystals are watching me in some way, tracking my interest. I can feel my face flushing with shame and confusion at what happened in the afternoon. I stop walking and clamp my legs together, remembering the harsh way she touched me, the restraints digging into my limbs. I try and push thoughts of Imogen to the back of my mind, conjuring a picture of my parents at the care center. Reminding myself what's at stake if I don't make everyone happy at Holistik. Especially, apparently, myself.

There is a home a few streets from Holistik with a Bösendorfer piano. I followed the sound one day until I found it, pressed up by the window, which they often leave open. Either they are rich enough to keep the piano in good condition, or they are ignorant about humidity's ability to slowly degrade the giant wooden instruments. I've heard of pianos in Florida that drowned above water.

A young girl has her piano lessons in the early evenings, and it has become a habit to stroll by and listen. Tonight she is learning a piece I also studied as a kid. As I watch her, I briefly wonder if I am a ghost, haunting a life I once had. She stops playing occasionally to push the little black curls from her face with her pudgy hands. My fingers start to itch, and I feel like I might cry, remembering the hours I had spent at the piano with the music of my father's voice in my ear. I start walking to stop my mind from thinking too much about the past. I have learned to keep going even when I can't be sure of what will come after.

CHAPTER ELEVEN

The next night, Helen is waiting for me when I arrive. In loose jeans and a cream oversized sweater, her beauty is devastating.

"Come on, Goose!" She calls as we walk in together, and a small furry creature tears across the frosted-over yard and through the door. She gestures for me to sit at a long wooden dining room table, so polished it looks like a mirror. I agonized over my makeup and clothing, but I still look out of place at the table set with expensive, albeit mismatched, porcelain and china.

"May I?" I ask Helen. I extend a hand to Goose, who immediately jumps from the chair onto my legs. I stroke the dog's silky coat and enjoy how it warms my lap. "She?"

Helen nods.

"She is so sweet."

Goose lets out a lengthy whine, making us laugh.

"She's the best. Very spoiled, though. Gets her hair groomed at the Holistik dog spa once a month, courtesy of Uncle Victor. Admittedly, I coddle her a bit, too. Don't I, Goosie?"

On the table, Helen unveils a lamb roast with mint truffle

butter, roasted carrots in a ginger-honey glaze, a rich butternut squash soup with tangy blue cheese crumbles, and sourdough bread. I avoid eye contact with her as she explains the food and the processes by which she cooked everything. I'm afraid to show how moved I am, to be taken care of in this way. Apart from my parents, no one has ever cooked for me.

"This is unbelievably delicious," I say through a mouthful of bread. I had been anxious about using my utensils correctly, but Helen uses her hands for almost everything, and I follow suit.

"Thank you. I can't take all the credit, though. It's impossible to be a bad chef when your ingredients are this great. Everything came from the Organic Provisions farm in the Gunks."

"That's amazing. What is the farm like?"

She shrugs. "Typical farm. Produce. Lots of goats."

"I saw a video of it. The tour thing. All of the farmers look like models."

Helen looks at me sheepishly. "I'm pretty sure those were actually hired models."

"Oh."

"My uncle can be very particular about how his companies are represented. He thinks divorcing products from the labor they require is integral to increasing demand."

"Interesting. Why?"

"It apparently ruins the magic to know that real people are behind everything we do. Especially food. He got a lot of criticism for this interview where he said most people would be vegans if their food didn't come prepackaged with all signs of life removed. That's why the Holistik café is all about tasty shapes and colorful drinks."

"Tasty shapes," I murmur, distracted by the unique color and perfect heft of the cup in my hand.

"Do you like it? It's the same proprietary clay I use for the jars at Holistik."

"That's right, you make all of those!"

"I do! Well, not all of them anymore. The demand is pretty high, and it got to be impossible for one person. Also, I got so clumsy, I started dropping more jars than I could make!"

I reach for another piece of lamb, but Helen pulls the plate away. "You have to save room for dessert. I'll pack the lamb for you to take home, but I made a ton of ice cream and I need your help eating it."

She goes to the kitchen, and I look around, still not quite believing where I am. The walls are a moody dark blue, making the large space seem more intimate. Everything glows with the soft finish of care and ease. The spoons and forks are heavy, but tiny and delicate, for people who have never known the need to shovel food into their mouths. There is a small upright piano in the corner by a bookshelf full of leather-bound tomes. Beautiful raw walnut wood and well-maintained keys.

Behind me, the front door opens and shuts. I turn around and see Henry. My face burns with shame. Goose, who had been sleeping in my lap, pushes off, darting into a crevice between the bookcase and the piano. I sit very still, stupidly hoping he can't see me.

Helen comes back with bowls of light green ice cream. "You're home early. You remember each other?"

I wave a limp hand at Henry, but he stares at me blankly. He must think I'm crazy or obsessed with him, befriending his sister this way. If he even remembers me.

"Are you hungry? There's plenty of food."

"I ate with Uncle Vic."

"Henry, can you not stare?"

"I'm going to bed."

"OK, sleep well," Helen says as he clomps upstairs. "Goose, it's OK! Come out!" Helen beckons to Goose, who remains a hidden shadow. She sighs, giving up and rejoining me at the table. "She's been scared of Henry ever since we were little."

That explains Goose's absence the first time I was here.

"I'm sorry, I didn't even think about how weird it probably looks for me to be here," I whisper, embarrassed.

"No, it's not you. I'm sure he's just out of it. He's changed so much since he started working for Victor. He's always cranky and exhausted. Don't take it personally."

"What does he do?"

"I'm not entirely sure. He doesn't like to talk about it with me." She clears her throat. "How did you and Henry meet?"

I look down at my lap. "One of those apps."

"Oh," she says. Then adds quickly, "I'm not judging, honest. I'm just surprised. I didn't think Henry was into that kind of thing. He's so obsessed with his privacy and not using anything that could potentially be surveilled. Which app, if you don't mind my asking?"

"E-ros. God, it's so embarrassing." I attempt to laugh at myself, mortified.

Helen's brows try to connect over the expanse of her perfect temple. "It's not embarrassing. I've just never heard of that one. What's this one's shtick?"

"Hmm, I guess instead of swiping, you add people to your cart like it's a shopping app."

Spoken out loud, the app's premise sounds deranged.

Helen laughs. "Yeah, that totally tracks for where we've been heading as a society." She gestures at the bowl in front of me. "You haven't tried it."

I take a bite. Creamy and grassy. I instantly feel calmer and more awake.

"This is incredible. Mint?"

"Guess again." Helen points to the kitchen, where a giant Holistik canister sits on the counter, much larger than the receptacles sold at the store.

"Wow, I didn't know they came in different sizes."

"They don't . . . Promise you won't tell, but I sneak the bulk-size supplements from the Gunks when I'm out there. The formulas there have extra collagen, apparently." She winks at me, and the light freckles around her nose dance. "Victor probably wouldn't mind, but he can be a bit controlling when it comes to what people are and aren't imbibing. I'm sure you've noticed."

"Just a little," I say, laughing. "The other day, he was convinced that our skin looked too sallow from the store lights, so he had the bulbs changed, but also made us eat cubes of tallow for a radiant glow."

Helen rolls her eyes. "I've had those cubes."

"He was right, though! I looked way healthier after a few of them. I can't imagine . . . What's it like being related to him? I'm so curious about them."

"Who, Victor?"

"And Saje."

"Saje's story is kind of a sad one," Helen says, cupping her chin with a hand. "Not sure if you know, but she started the original Holistik store and was really struggling to keep it open after her husband left her with two infants and an insane amount of debt.

"I didn't know that. How awful."

"Yeah. He ran off with one of her employees, actually. So she was pretty crushed, of course, and was about to close the store when Victor and his ex-wife came in. Victor ended up paying her debts and supporting her family while he took over the store. Now the brand is bigger than she ever dreamed. She's practically family, too. I don't think there's anything she and Victor wouldn't do for each other.

"That's so kind of Victor."

"Isn't it? This is going to sound cheesy because I'm his family, but I really think he's incredible. He came from absolutely nothing and has somehow built this massive . . . well, empire. He has some funny ideas about things, sure, but he's one of the nicest people you'll meet. It's not just Saje, or people in his life. He really cares about making the world a more beautiful place. He's on every museum board, backs every major conservation effort. We have our differences, but what family doesn't?"

"Are you guys pretty close, then?" I ask.

"Definitely. I think he would like to be closer, like we were when I was a kid. I just need space sometimes. It was hard . . . Our parents weren't around too much, and Victor basically raised us. I'm very grateful for it, believe me."

"I'm sorry about your parents."

"Don't be. They're great, just preoccupied with living their lives. But yeah, really lucky we had Victor. He always made sure we were being taken care of, doing well in school, all that boring parent-y stuff."

"He must love you a lot."

"He does," she says softly.

"His face," I start to say, before I've realized what I'm saying. I try to rescue myself. "It's not quite—"

"Normal," she finishes for me. "He just can't help himself. He wants to be the first to try any new procedure, even when Saje tells him it needs more testing. The guy has had years of minke whale collagen injections, Silkie sternal cartilage grafts, and god knows what else."

"Cartilage grafts? That sounds so painful. Why?"

Helen stares at me uncomprehendingly.

"Why does he get these things done?" I ask again.

"He wants to be beautiful. Like everyone who walks into Holistik, right? Maybe everyone in the world?"

I try not to laugh out loud. What could the girl in front of me possibly know about wanting to be beautiful?

"Was he always like this?"

"Always. For other people, too. Like, when I was a kid. If he was coming over to visit, he would send someone to do my hair and makeup before his arrival. For my eighth birthday, he had his favorite designer make their entire fall line in my size. I realize how privileged this sounds, but all I wanted was to dress like everyone else at my school, and instead, I had teeny suits and blazers!"

She notices my expression. "He wouldn't tell me what to wear now, of course. That's definitely one of the things we've worked on in the last few years. It's not really his fault. His beliefs and taste are so developed, you know? I needed time . . . still need it, to figure out my own."

She seems embarrassed. Defensive, even. I worry I've overstepped by asking her too much about her family. I try to lighten the mood. "If only we'd known each other. I would have traded my crusty secondhand clothing for your clothes any day!"

It sounds sadder than I had intended, but she smiles, and relief pours through my body.

"So how are you getting along with Lilith? She's your manager, right?"

"Lilith is . . . nice."

Helen laughs, breaking the residual tension. "Now that's a lie! Lilith has never been nice, but she is a great person. She'll warm up to you, it just takes time. She's very insular, which can come across as unfriendly. I think she tries to be a little repellent. If she didn't, people would never leave her alone. She can be really charming."

A pang of jealousy. I've never had to worry about too many people liking me. "Have you known her for a long time?"

"Do you want some more wine? We should have more wine."

She gets up quickly and returns with an opened bottle. "We kind of grew up together. Her adoptive parents are both famous photographers. They traveled the world covering civil wars and geopolitics. She was over a lot. Victor and my aunts, my parents when they were around . . . they all kind of looked after her. She and I were very close."

Helen leans back in her seat and tucks her knees under her chin, hugging them. She looks so vulnerable, I have to stop myself from reaching for her hand.

"Are you still close?" I find myself holding my breath while I wait for an answer.

"We are now, but there were a few years where I was sure we would never be friends again."

"What happened?"

"I'm not sure. I don't think it was personal? As she got older, I think she had a harder time with her biological dad. When her mom died, he chose to give her up for adoption instead of taking her in. He checked in sometimes, but mostly he wanted to focus on his films. Her resentment toward him grew and grew, especially since the parents who adopted her hardly traveled less. It cemented the idea that art is something only selfish people pursue. She got so intense. Self-righteous.

"She thought it was stupid that I wanted to study art history. Accused me of leaning into an already too-privileged life. At first it seemed like she wanted to push me in a good way, but it was so persistent. In the end, she said terrible things about me and my family. Unforgivable things. And, of course, she had grown up with us. She had quite the arsenal of ugly truths to throw in our faces."

"That sounds ungrateful," I say, trying to somehow telegraph that I would never do anything like that to her.

Helen shakes her head. "No, no, it wasn't like that. We didn't expect or need her to be grateful. We happily treated her as part of the family. She was the one who started to distance herself. She even accused her own adoptive parents of not doing enough, of just taking pretty photos of people suffering. There was a particularly nasty interview where she said that her parents were profiting from humanitarian disasters by allowing their work to be shown in cultural magazines and expensive exhibits. It broke their hearts. But anyway, that's why she went to journalism school. She wanted to make a difference. We didn't talk for those four years. It didn't seem like she would ever forgive us for not living up to her ideals."

"I'm sorry, Helen."

She is quiet for a moment, gazing at the candles on the table. Fingers of wax slide into a saucer.

"That's why it's so weird."

"What is?"

"After journalism school, she came back, and it's like nothing ever happened. She never talks about any of the things she used to care about and refers to it all as a phase she regrets. She's even managing Manhattan's Holistik, which, let's face it, is kind of the most frivolous thing. She used to butt heads with Victor all the time because she found that whole world problematic."

"You think Holistik is frivolous?" I ask, surprised.

She dips her fingers in the dripping wax and rubs. "I think all things should strive to be sustainable and ethical. In that sense, Holistik is great. It's obviously better than toxic beauty products that negatively impact people and our planet. But the whole business of wellness can feel a little too self-important."

"Wait, do you not think eyeshadow in a bamboo case is going to save the world?" I pretend to be shocked.

"Exactly! And does anyone really need new eyeshadow? It isn't our fault, of course. Buying stuff is supposed to make us happy. It's a Band-Aid slapped on top of structural issues that actually need to be addressed. My point is, there are real and serious needs, and businesses should be striving to serve those instead of trying to manufacture new ones."

"Does Victor know how you feel about this?"

"Definitely not. His whole business model privileges the already privileged. Those who can spend exorbitant amounts of time and money on self-care and making themselves beautiful."

I say it before I can stop myself. "A lot of the clients are very rich, that's true. And there are a lot of people who just want to be beautiful. Should they be doing better things with their time? Maybe. Could they? For sure. But many of them are young women. They don't necessarily have much money, but they spend what they can spare on bettering themselves. Maybe what we're doing is manipulative, but maybe it's important, too. I can't see where that difference begins or ends. Beauty has always been one of the only ways women have been able to access power, and I can't fault any of them for wanting more of it."

Truthfully, I relate to the young women more than I want to admit and feel a bit defensive about Holistik, the first place that has afforded me real and social currency.

"I don't really expect you to understand," I add hastily.

Helen's eyebrows shoot up in surprise and my heart skips a beat.

"Why wouldn't I understand?" she asks.

I stare down at the ice cream, unable to meet her gaze.

When I look back up, she is smiling faintly into space.

"I hadn't thought of it that way before," she says, starting to laugh lightly. "No wonder Victor and Saje love you. You're fully drinking the Kool-Aid."

"So what do you think would save the world? If not the vast and marketable venture that is sustainable beauty and wellness?" I ask, eager to change the subject.

In the candlelight, Helen's gaze is soft as it rests on the piano for a few long seconds.

"I'm not one of those people who thinks music is going to save the world or whatever. But I do think art is one of the only things that can help people get in touch with the part of themselves and the world that's worth saving."

Her eyes flick back to mine, and I feel so pinned down by her attention I find it hard to breathe.

"Enough about me. Why don't you play anymore?"

I had been hoping to avoid this question. I look down at my hands where they are strangling a napkin and take a deep breath. "The last time I played, my parents came to watch." My arms are getting the tingly sensation they always get when I remember anything too close to this moment. "I asked them to stay longer after the concert. By the time they drove home, it was late and they had—" I spread my fingers on the solid underside of the table to steady them. "I haven't been able to play since. I love it. I miss it. But I can't sit down without remembering."

"I'm sorry," she whispers.

I finger the chain around my neck, wondering if I'll have to spend time in the chair tomorrow to make up for these recollections.

Her eyes, searching for mine, seem capable of reading my thoughts. "If you coat the mandala with Vaseline or anything that has petroleum or lanolin, it keeps your stats at a base normal and basically only functions as a reminder for your supplements."

I force my mouth into a smile and look down at my lap.

"I'm sorry if this is too forward," she says, taking a deep breath, "but it doesn't help anyone, especially your parents, to punish yourself."

She gets up and starts to clear the plates. I stop pressing my hands under the table and let them shake wildly. She is right, of course, but even if I wanted to play, it is impossible. I tried after the incident. Every day, I sat at the piano, only to have my arms remain at my sides. The black commas between keys seemed to spill over until I was eventually swallowed by the shadow of my grief. Maybe the muscle memory I had worked so hard to develop at the piano was now too adept, remembering only trauma. I know that if I were to put my hands on the instrument, they would miss the keys entirely, playing only the dark spaces between.

Helen starts taking things into the kitchen, and as soon as she is out of view, I reach into my mouth and take out what my teeth could not cut through in the ice cream. A small yellow-white sliver, heavy in my palm. I slip it into my pocket. When she comes back, she has a small tub with her. She sits next to me and slowly reaches a hand down my collar. I can almost feel flames engulfing my cheeks. She retrieves my mandala and brings it toward her, pulling us close. My body simmers as she carefully rubs the silver object with Vaseline, our foreheads almost touching. Our thighs reach for each other through stiff denim, and I'm certain my hair is lifting from my scalp, inching forward to entwine with hers. She must be able to read the longing in my face, feel my heart thrashing erratically just beneath her fingertips when she touches the mandala to my clavicle.

"You'll have to reapply in a day or two, but that should do the trick for now," she says, getting up.

I start to panic as I realize the night is coming to an end. I don't want this to be the last time we see each other, but I don't know how to ask for more of her time. I search the room, looking for an excuse, and find one.

"Do *you* still play?"

Helen laughs. "It's been years, and I was terrible then, even with consistent practice."

I try hard to keep the desperation in my voice to a minimum.

"If you ever wanted to start again, I'd be happy to help. It would be fun, maybe even therapeutic for me, to have an excuse to be around a piano again."

We begin to see each other almost weekly for piano lessons. I come over after work to find her already at the piano, hands spread wide on the keys. I sit down next to her, giving her pointers, assigning her scales and exercises. I love sharing the piano bench with her, love the way she leans into me when I make her laugh. It surprises me to learn that I am funny, that there are things people could like about me that have nothing to do with my being a good pianist or working at Holistik. Besides my parents, she is the first person to make me feel valuable for who I am, not what I do. I had forgotten that I have worth beyond the care I can offer my parents. She had been right that first dinner. I didn't think I deserved a life outside of that duty. Now, after three long years, it feels terrifying and wonderful to begin thinking that maybe I do. I can never bring myself to touch the piano, but sometimes I go as far as putting my hands over hers for demonstrations. I often stay after our lessons for dinner. We cook and eat, and if it gets late, I stay over in the guest bedroom. When I leave, I am always afraid it will be the last time I see her.

Helen and Lilith frequently see each other, and after a few weeks of piano lessons, Helen starts inviting me to spend time with them. I always say yes, even though I can sense that Lilith doesn't love my company. I can't remotely afford to keep up with their lifestyle, so I look and never buy, which doesn't matter; there's nothing I want more than the joy of being seen with them anyway. We shop in Soho, brunch in Williamsburg, grab coffee and wander galleries on the Lower East Side. We eat out constantly, everywhere from a place in Bushwick that only serves pink food to the soft opening for a new restaurant concept by Victor—the Gilded Ant, which prepares only raw insects. I've never seen so much of the city, and I begin to realize that there exist many New York Citys . . . it is endless and endlessly changing. It means something different to everyone. It should comfort me to see that there are so many spaces where I might belong, but I don't want to find where I belong; I want to *become* someone who belongs next to Helen and Lilith, in all the spaces they occupy. I often walk behind them, watching their hips move in unison, their hair tangling down their backs, Helen's mane as bright and curly as Lilith's is dark and straight. It never seems like there's room for me, but then there is Helen extending a hand, pulling out an extra chair, hanging up my coat.

Lilith and I never see each other alone, except for one time, by accident. I was taking my customary walk after work, going farther this time because I saw a woman who looked so much like Ma from the back, my breath hitched. I followed her for a while, noticing how similarly she walked and dressed, the same worn sandals with a broken leather strap and even a similar vulnerable slant to her neck. Her small strong hands were twined in the straps of a few plastic bags heavy with produce. They looked so like Ma's, I tried to get closer. Would her fingertips be callused from the piano? Would she have the same gentle smile with closed lips, a determined look in her eyes? It was suddenly imperative that I see her face. I started walking faster, and that was when I ran into Lilith. I stumbled, catching myself on an older woman in a wheelchair. I mumbled an apology and tried to extricate myself.

"Are you OK?" Lilith asked me.

My leg was stuck in one of the woman's tote bags. Lilith bent down and helped to untangle me as my eyes frantically searched for the woman I had been following. I couldn't see her anywhere, and tears arrived in my eyes so quickly, it was as if I had been slapped. An anguished sound escaped my throat.

Lilith spoke in another language to the woman in the wheelchair before turning to me.

"What are you doing in Chinatown?"

"I was just taking a walk." I hadn't realized I was in Chinatown at all. My eyes still stung with tears.

Lilith looked at me with concern. "I was just about to make some tea, why don't you come in and warm up?"

I followed her as she wheeled the older woman into a small apartment.

"Do you mind waiting here for a second? I'm going to get her settled in."

They were gone a long time. When Lilith came back, she looked drained. I poured a cup of tea for her.

"Thanks. My grandmother . . . she's not well. She always thinks I'm my mother and I don't have the heart to tell her otherwise."

I nodded in sympathy and gestured around before asking, "Do you live here, too?"

Lilith shook her head. "In fact, I should be getting back to my place."

"Of course."

I rinsed my cup in the sink and collected my things.

At the doorway, Lilith stopped me.

She tucked a strand of hair behind my ear.

"You're really pretty," she said with surprise, as if seeing me for the first time.

I forced a laugh that came out as a weak chuckle.

"Really. It's easy to forget. At Holistik. I see it all the time with the other girls, so I'm telling you now. You're beautiful."

She looked at me with utter seriousness, and all I could see was the perfect symmetry of her face. My parents always told me I was beautiful growing up, often play-fighting over which features of mine came from them. No one else, until now, has ever had anything nice to say about the way I look. There was an entryway mirror behind her, and I stared into it as she put her shoes on. I tried to see what she saw, but I couldn't.

The next day, she went back to more or less ignoring me in the store and during the time we spent with Helen. So much so that I've half convinced myself I manufactured the whole encounter.

Where Lilith is hot and cold, Helen is always and only warm. She is, I suppose, my first friend. I study her the way an overeager student studies a poem, committing it to memory because comprehension is out of reach. I learn of her interests and try to make them my own. She loves to draw and read and watch soccer. She loves running early in the morning and staying up late to sketch, often falling asleep covered in sooty black pencil, dreams secreting ink. I buy a pair of cheap running shoes to accompany her on runs and carry a small black notebook in case I am hit with artistic inspiration.

It doesn't take long for her to start confiding in me. Everything from small family spats to the self-consciousness she has about her appearance, knowing no matter what she does, she will garner attention. She isn't wrong. The baggy linen clothing she wears does nothing to lessen the lure of her body. If anything, people are more intrigued by her inscrutability. She pulls her hair into a stiff bun every morning, hoping it'll be less noticeable that way. It never cooperates; one curl will fall, then another and another until her head is surrounded in a halo of bright banana fluff.

The first few months of our friendship, I wait for a crack in the facade. A moment of imperfection, or at least banality. It never arrives. The light blue veins that braid her translucent wrists are perfect Ming replicas. Her ears are porcelain seashells, snatched from some unlucky naiad; her irises are the gray blue of a cornflower dipped swiftly in ink. Even the tiny brushstrokes that make up her eyebrows seem hand-drawn, exquisite.

One night, I arrive home late to an awful stench. I reluctantly step through the front door and put my bag down, trying to get a sense of where the smell might be coming from.

"Oh, good, you're home!" Alice walks over to me. "What . . . is happening right now?" she says, tilting her head.

I look down at myself and realize I'm covered head to toe in yellow pollen. "Trying out a new treatment."

"Like, you want to see how bad your allergies can get?"

"Holistik is collaborating with Wolfgang Laib for his new exhibit. We're going to have a pop-up booth at MoMA offering services."

"Ooh, what are they?"

"So far there's a pollen glow bath, a Burmese lacquer laser treatment, and a meditation ritual in a milkstone tub. Wolfgang himself is pouring milk on the clients."

"Any chance you can hook me up with a freebie?"

"I can try and add you to the trial list, but it's already hundreds of people long and I don't think I can do anything beyond that. Sorry," I add unhelpfully.

Alice's face falls with disappointment.

"What's that smell?" I ask, partially to distract her.

"I've been cleansing the aura of the house. You're the only thing left."

I stand still in the living room and let Alice holler at me as she throws a mixture of things at me from a dirty Ace Hardware bucket. As she circles me in a bizarre crab walk, I can't help but feel moved by the gesture. Even if she doesn't succeed in expelling my demons or whatever, the fact that she wants to is touching.

When I get downstairs, I check my email and see a couple from Applebaum sent in quick succession. My heart starts racing. I read the words a few times to fully understand.

My phone slips to the floor and I fall onto the bed. My parents are doing better. One email includes a scanned copy of the assessment from the consulting doctor. I lie there in a daze as the words run through my head. *Recovering remarkably. Will just take some more time. Full cognitive recovery possible.* I hold on to the good words. Leave behind the ones like *significant physical recovery unlikely.* I will think about those later.

CHAPTER TWELVE

The incidents began imperceptibly. The first one I remember took place on the subway. I sat down and wrapped my tattered winter coat around myself. It had snowed that morning, for the first time, and the subway was crowded with people staggering under their heavy coats and just-purchased holiday gifts. A man was staring at me while rubbing himself over his pants. The people around us pointed their eyes elsewhere and I tried to look away, too, but I could see him no matter where I turned. I saw everything about him with brilliant microscopic vision: the cracks in his hands from the cold and the small crocodile logo on his stained shirt. It was as if the frame of my vision had been stretched wider. It was even difficult to blink: I simply didn't need to. I kept my eyes open, counting to myself to see how long I could go, blinking only when I felt alarmed by how many minutes were passing. I squeezed my eyes shut and pressed them with the backs of my hands a few times. When I opened them, I caught a glimpse of my reflection in the subway doors before exiting. My face was warped in the murky glass and my eyes had tripled in size.

As I ran off the train, I could see all the way behind me. I started blinking as soon as I stopped thinking about it, and when I got home, my face looked normal in the mirror.

One morning just before New Year's, I slid off my deflating mattress and kneed myself in the face. I had been thinning out for a while, but this was different. My legs had seemingly grown longer overnight. The gentle slopes of my mother's body had disappeared from my frame as if someone had lopped them off. My legs stayed long and lean for a week before I understood the change was permanent. The new stretched-out limbs look so fragile to me, I am sometimes afraid of moving too fast and running into something that will pierce my delicate papyrus skin or crush my bones, which are now as slender, as vulnerable, as flower stems. There is no longer any way to deny it. I am becoming my best self.

For many months, looking in the mirror has led to surprise. Surprise, my skin has lightened, and my sunspots have been chased away. Surprise, I am so thin, in the mirror, I see geometric shapes, a cubist rendition of who I used to be. My breasts, on the other hand, have swelled, are as padded as a freshman's first essay. Surprise, my skin is fantastically elastic thanks to Holistik's extra-strength collagen. Surprise, my limp straight hair has thickened and curled, and the hair at my roots is many degrees lighter. My lips steadily inflate, reminding me of the air mattress I sleep on every night. Surprise, there seems to be construction on my nose bridge, but how can that be? I write it off, pretend I'm overworked and it's making me crazy. The truth is, I barely recognize the lithe woman looking back at me in the mirror. I have started to obtain the glow the other girls at the store have. The luster I assumed came from privilege and a trust fund. Whatever I have been taking is buffing away the grime of an ordinary existence from the outside in.

I offer to share it all with Alice, who, while friendlier than ever, remains petulantly jealous. But maybe because the products are all tailored to me, they have no effect on her besides making her violently ill. She experiments with dosages, not seeming to mind the constant trembling and lack of bodily control that signify her body's rejection, but I can't bear to watch her go through it. After her third fall down the stairs, I confiscate everything. Her reactions give me pause, but I keep taking my assigned supplements because they all seem to work fine for me. Better than fine, if I'm being honest. Alice has to watch as the dirty downstairs basement room becomes a magic cocoon from which I emerge each day brighter and more incandescent than the last. I even woke up once, in the middle of the night, from a glare that turned out to be the opalescence of my skin.

January is a whirlwind at Holistik with the launch of a new procedure. Holistik has patented the use of the *Turritopsis nutricula* jellyfish's transdifferentiating cells to clinically reverse aging. The phone rings incessantly, and celebrities fly in from all over the world for the facial shots. The injections take only a few minutes, but we have to monitor the patients for over six hours afterward in case their bodies reject the treatment. Only a handful of times do the women start to seize in their chairs. Each time, Lilith runs for the doctor while I wipe the patient's foaming mouth and try my best to keep them calm. I was told later they settled out of court quietly with the promise of free procedures in the future. The women who had negative reactions were all left with a slight sheen on their faces, a reticulating pattern only visible in a certain light.

On Valentine's Day, we launch a mascara made with a rare sea algae engineered to enhance lash growth. It is truly a miracle product. With one swipe, my stubby straight lashes thicken and fan, reaching an impossible length. When I wash it off at night, the new length and curl stay. In the quiet moments before falling asleep, I think I can even hear the rustle of them growing. I dream of lying on a white field where elaborate snowflakes float down and coat my body, landing on my lashes and clouding my vision. Each flake webs and sticks, a beautiful fur metastasizing. I try to open my eyes, but my lids are too heavy. They are covered by a forest of light feathers, layer upon layer of dim wood.

The next day, I wake in a panic. The skin under my eyebrows has stretched, and I have to manually open my eyes. Holding the sagging flesh with one hand, I quickly message Lilith and Saje on the Holistik employee app and let them know I can't make my shift because of a health emergency. I'm working up the courage to go upstairs and ask Alice for a clinic recommendation when Lilith's name flashes across my phone screen.

"Let me guess, your eyes won't open?"

I take a car to work and sit quietly behind a pair of large sunglasses. When I get to the store, Lilith is waiting. She shows me in the mirror how to massage the extra skin under my brow until it softens into a gel-like texture. Then she coaxes it to fold over itself, creating a crevice and tucking it in. I'm surprised by the gentleness with which she helps me.

"The first few days are always weird. It'll be stiff when you wake up, but do everything I showed you and it'll be automatic by next week."

She leaves me in the bathroom, and I look in the mirror at my astonished reflection. Upstairs, I fill the expanded real estate above my eyes with a light blue eyeshadow made from lepidopteran powder. Even with my eyes open wide, the product is visible.

Every girl who looked like me at the Conservatory had procured a surgery to achieve these results. I could never have afforded it, but now it would be superfluous.

It snows the whole day. By the time I leave the store, the city is covered by a crisp white sheet. When I get home, Alice is sitting alone in the dark, drinking a glass of red wine.

"Did you get eyelash extensions?" she asks, her eyes narrowing with suspicion.

I reach up and touch my newly lengthened eyelashes. "No. Not really."

"Oh, please." She's slurring her words. "You're trying to convince me those are natural?" She gets up, closing the gap between us surprisingly fast. "Something's different. Wrong. I sensed it in the cleanse."

She's very close to me. Close enough to take my face into her hands, cupping each side with a hot palm. Her eyes are glazed over, unfocused.

"Do you want to fuck Charlie?"

"No."

So she has also noticed Charlie watching me, more often than usual and longer than appropriate.

Her bottom lip starts to tremble, and I begin to feel bad for her. Her eyes water, and what must be seventy coats of mascara run down her face.

I step away, but her grip on me is firm.

"Hey, relax! I just want to look at you." She starts laughing and shaking me, a misguided attempt to make me feel at ease.

Her face is so close now, I wonder for a split second if she's going to kiss me. I hear myself yelping as I hit the ground. White flashes dance in front of me and sirens reverberate in my head. I press on my left eye to stem the pain.

Alice returns to her wine, sitting down at the dining table to spread the eyelashes she has pulled from me in a straight line.

The next day, Lilith is staring at me with her mouth slightly open. "Did you not massage it like I showed you?" Her bangs are swept to one side and her forehead is very smooth. I wonder if it has ever moved.

"This is unrelated."

She looks at me unconvinced.

"Roommate drama," I finally say, rolling my one good eye. She seems equal parts horrified and impressed.

"Do you live with MMA fighters or something? Here, we're sold out of this, but we have some in a tester."

Lilith takes me to a drawer and pulls out a balm to put on my eye. It's in a white Holistik jar, but I don't recognize the product. The label reads *Blattodea Healing Balm*.

"Blattodea. What is it?" I ask, dabbing a bit on my finger. I haven't learned about this product yet.

"Just trust me," she says.

The pain isn't terrible, but Alice had gotten me with a spangled nail, bursting a few blood vessels. It looks worse than it feels. I had left home as early as possible to avoid giving her the satisfaction of seeing the damage she had caused. Madison comes over to us, looking concerned.

"Maybe you should work downstairs today?" She looks at me apologetically with her wide bland features. "Sorry, it's just, you look totally mulched, and we literally sell beauty."

She flounces away under Lilith's icy stare.

"She's so insensitive. You know her first year here, she made an anonymous petition against my being manager?"

"She did? Why?" I ask.

"I won't take certain hair supplements or use any of the natural bleaches. My dark hair color is one of the only things I have that connects me to my biological mom. I know it makes me somewhat of an anomaly here, but obviously Saje and Victor are fine with it, so she should fuck off."

I nod my agreement but volunteer to go downstairs anyway when a customer enters the store and flinches at the sight of me. Madison watches me smugly as I walk toward the stairs.

The same age I am, Madison was a ballet dancer at one of the dance companies funded by Victor. She has been at Holistik ever since she aged out of ballet in her mid-twenties. Though she has worked here for a few years, she still struggles with the intense memorization needed for products, ingredients, and uses. I have been memorizing complex piano music from an early age, so it comes easily to me. I never mean to show off, but the commission system breeds competition. My good memory and the fact that I was "handpicked" by Saje from a "shithole diner in *Midtown*" make me an easy target for resentment.

When I get downstairs, I unpack, catalog, and shelve products. Time passes slowly until, without warning, six people in white hazmat suits come down the stairs and walk to the Zoo. They are carrying weapons with them, intimidating rifles, and underneath their papery protective garments, they are wearing camouflage. Victor and Saje arrive a little after, not noticing me between the shelves.

"I don't know why we keep trying with other animals when the octopus and gibbon are perfectly viable. I mean, how are we going to explain this to the conservancy board? The last thing we need is more rumors." Saje sounds anxious as they hurry down the stairs.

They both look disheveled, less put together than I have ever seen them. Saje looks to have been interrupted mid-pedicure. Her bloated feet are shoved in a pair of disposable orange flip-flops and covered in a film of dirt or oil. Victor's pale eyes are bloodshot, and his light hair hangs like clumps of noodles with a garnish of leftover dandruff.

"We've come so far from Bedford's research at Cornell, we can't stop now. We haven't even had a feasible zygote! I'll take care of the board," he whispers reassuringly to Saje as they walk briskly into the Zoo. "We owe this to our families," he adds quietly.

I pass a few hours alone with the troubling image of hazmat suits and weapons replaying in my mind. I can't hear anything from the Zoo, and no one returns to the employee area. Lilith comes down eventually, looking for me.

"What's going on with the hazmat suits?" I can't resist asking her.

"I'm not sure. Something with the animals."

"Are they OK?"

"I don't know and I'm not asking. You shouldn't either. It's better to stay out of things that don't directly involve us. People have been let go for getting too curious."

Her face is sealed of all expression. I nod and try to emulate her impassiveness.

"Hey, so you'll be on your own tonight for a couple's treatment. Are you going to be all right?"

"Isn't Madison still here?"

"She had some emergency again. Had to leave." She fakes vomiting. We both know the emergency was Madison's new mystery boyfriend.

"I'll be fine, I know how to close up. And they've prepaid, right?"

"Right. I don't think you've prepped for this procedure before, though, so I'll take you through it now before my shift ends."

Lilith walks with me to a corner of the inventory shelving and removes an enormous tub. "This is compost from the Gunks farm."

"Compost? So, like, dirt."

"Yeah, but from the Gunks, so it's basically liquid gold. And you know how Victor feels about waste. Better to find a use for it. So first, you'll dump all of this into the soaking chambers. And make sure the infrared lights are on. The worms can't handle anything brighter."

She takes down a gold pitchfork hanging from the wall. It hits a shelf nearby, making a beautiful ringing sound.

"Use this to sift gently before and after the procedure. Don't worry if you see things that haven't fully broken down. Sometimes animals get in there and drown if they get in too deep. We had to throw away an entire bin once because the scent was so terrible, no one could stand to be down here. Turned out to be some animal too big for the worms to process."

I nod, hoping desperately to myself that I won't encounter any large remains.

"And feed them after . . . there's butter lettuce and mashed persimmon in the fridge."

"Are Victor and Saje going to be here until after closing?"

"They're already gone. They left a couple of hours ago."

Lilith is halfway up the stairs when she turns back to me, waiting.

"What?" I ask her.

She looks at me for another moment before shaking her head. "It's nothing. It's—" She bites her lip. "This couple might . . . be loud during the procedure. They're Victor's friends, so we kind of let them do whatever they want. Don't be scared, you'll be totally safe. You can text or call my number if you need help. If you hear anything, it's probably fine, just don't look too closely at the monitor."

I recognize the couple. They're regulars, often shopping and partaking in services at Holistik. The man is an art dealer or collector or both, and quite handsy with all the store girls. He puts an ever-lowering palm on our backs and tries to show us fine art on his phone, which doesn't have enough pixels and which he doesn't know how to use anyway. We have to coo at everything he shows us while also trying to squirm away. Saje will periodically walk by and give us a big wink as if to say, *You are such a minx flirting on the job, but I adore you, so I'll look the other way.*

He pushes his partner to get more treatments all the time. While he waits for her, he does the same bit where he compares our technicians to fine art restorers before he segues into his appreciation for things, like our youth, that don't need to be restored. I feel sorry for his partner. While he flirts with us, she's doing everything she can to maintain his interest. Weekly vernix facial wraps, a treatment that, besides looking and smelling awful, costs thousands of dollars per session. Monthly stoma vacuum sealing, which closes her pores. The ones that remain, she enlarges and embeds with diamonds so that, upon first glance, she looks to be freckled with the cosmos. She gets the same orthodontic procedure that Saje gets to maintain her Madonna tooth gap. She even gets a pubic hair transplant every few weeks, one of our most painful procedures, exchanging her natural coarse hairs for mink implants.

I have never been alone in the store at night. The couple's procedure is a few hours long, past when the store is closed to the public, and when I finish everything that needs to be done, I allow myself the indulgence of taking a bath in the employee restroom.

I fill the bottom with salts and set an alarm for an hour before their procedure ends. The temperature is perfect when I slip into the water. The steam coils thickly around me, bringing the scented salts, hand-mixed by Sloane, into contrasting focus. Wet bark and fresh cedar mixes with musk and lime blossom.

A sigh escapes me, then another. I pause and realize the sighing isn't coming from me but from the camera in the main employee space. I had turned the volume up, in case the couple needed anything, so I could quickly get out of the bath to meet their requests, if necessary. The man is grunting now and groaning. It sounds painful. Reluctantly, I press a towel to my body and hurry outside.

Lilith had said not to look, but what if someone needs help? He is just finishing as I reach the monitor. I watch as she fills with his spume and something else. Plump white larvae wriggling blindly over her sticky mink mons. She reaches down and takes a handful of the mixture and brings it to his mouth. I return to my bath, sinking my head underwater, trying and failing to wash away what I just witnessed.

"Thank you," they whisper to me as they leave the room streaked in dirt. Everyone feels the need to lower their voices when the infrared lights are on.

I wait for the front door chime to signal their exit before I start combing the dirt with the golden pitchfork. I throw in the mashed persimmon and butter lettuce for the worms and watch as they twitch in ecstasy. The air is humid from the couple's efforts, and I sweat as I move the dirt around, wondering if I should throw it away.

The front door chimes again. I still my breath and stop sifting. With the pitchfork in hand, I walk quietly down the hallway of the spa to the main store area. The space is quiet and shadows yawn from the gloomy entrance.

Smoke drifts lazily from the candles I blew out earlier, and a patch of light comes from the staircase. The unctuous creams and oils have lost their luster and look like ghostly tubs of grease and stiff gray paste. I lock the front door and go back to the spa room, dumping the dirt in its tub.

I hear something else. The soaking chambers still need to be rinsed, but I decide to go home right away. I consider leaving my things, but realize I need my MetroCard, my keys, what little money I have. The store is still when I pass through it to go downstairs. I take the stairs slowly, heart spasming, and tighten my fingers around the gold pitchfork. The light is on, thankfully, but something is off.

A sickly green haze fills the room, and something bitter and acrid stings my eyes. There is muck in the atmosphere, a green dust clinging to the bulbs. It gets denser as I walk back toward the closet to grab my things. The bathroom door is closed, and no light shines from beneath the door. I could have sworn I had left the light on and the door open to dispel the humidity from my bath. I start to head upstairs but notice a green glow on the floor in front of the Zoo.

Whatever is dispersing the green powder is coming from that direction. Only lab assistants and researchers have access to the Zoo, but the usually padlocked door is ajar, the biometric lock screen disabled. I can't help it; I walk over and push the door open further.

Snakes float in glowing green tanks that line the walls like blank TVs in a deserted electronics superstore. The automated water-circulation systems are going berserk. The snakes are slamming their bloated bodies into the glass repeatedly. Fish crowd together on their sides in dense cloudy water. The glassy eyes of an ocelot shine from where it is keeled over in a cage. Baby gibbons lie in a heap, piled high in the corner of a large transparent cell. A monkey covered in vomit is sitting, unconscious or dead, in its own shit.

A deep resonance clangs as the pitchfork drops from my hand to the floor. I run out, throwing up in my hands, a sticky white albumen coating matted yellow fur. Something red and spiky. What did I eat? I hear a terrible scrape and footsteps behind me, picking up rhythm. I turn too late.

CHAPTER THIRTEEN

The stars move at an alarming rate. Like a finger is in the sky, scrolling endlessly. I try to get up, but I don't have control of my limbs. My mouth is open, and I can't quite close it all the way. It's filled with something soft and moist. Trees froth beside me while an engine purrs beneath. A preacher and a singer from the '80s each try their best to perforate a light veil of static. I breathe in the scent of pine and gasoline before closing my eyes.

My chest convulses, waking me. The mandala is overheating, creating a burning sensation on my skin. I flip it open and ingest the pills, coughing them down dry. I am lying on the ground by a large bed, surrounded by floor-to-celing glass windows. A family of deer watches me from a few feet away. Someone has clothed me in a long-sleeved white dress, but I am shivering with cold. A chair by the bed has a green scarf draped over it. I loop it around my neck. The deer continue to look at me. Their blank stares make me uneasy. Occasionally they make small jerky movements at the neck, like they are glitching. My bag is on the floor by my feet. I pick it up and get my phone out. No service.

Nothing to do but tour the premises.

Dark leather couches shimmer like caviar in a bed of pale stone surfaces. The ceiling is high and wood-beamed, giving the place a bright and spacious feel. To the left of the living room, I see a kitchen island that is probably bigger than many real islands, and to the right, an eating area with a dining table that must have necessitated the sacrifice of a small forest.

Like in the bedroom, the walls are glass, giving me the illusion of being uncovered in the woods. Needles of sunlight stab through the dense surrounding foliage, suffusing everything with warmth. Hot steam curls above a pool beyond the dining room. A sudden hiss makes me jump. A dark gray cat glares at me for stepping on its tail and disappears through a door to my left.

I follow the cat into a nearly identical bedroom. But instead of a bed, a giant glass dome lies in the center. The rounded top rises high above me, and the circular base takes up almost the entire room. The surface is hypnotic—layered with spherical grooves like rings on a tree. Maybe a sculpture of an alien vessel, or a mysterious mercury droplet from space.

The mirror distorts me, fracturing my reflection. The cat yawns at itself in the glass and comes back to me, nuzzling my legs. It goes back to the dome, using its claws to pull at something from underneath. I get on my knees and try to see what it could be. Too close. The cat hisses at me again and runs out of the room, leaving the long copper threads it has pawed out from under the mirror. I touch the plasticky strands. Maybe hair from a cheap wig.

There is a narrow desk in the corner where papers are neatly stacked. I go over to look at them. List after list of names, all of them traditionally female. One of them is mine, with a check-mark next to the words *good candidate for Skintellect and Everlasting*. Others are good or bad candidates for more words I don't recognize. A loud sound makes me drop the papers. A deer attempting to walk through the window, repeatedly jabbing its right hoof. It shows no recognition of being obstructed. I leave the room, unnerved by its behavior.

Out in the living room, I hear loud rustling. A repeated howl. I walk toward the sound, beyond the kitchen and the living room. The whooshing gets louder, joined by a grating sound reminiscent of nails being dragged on metal. In a low voice, a woman is speaking.

"Well, look who's awake!"

Saje looks surprised to see me.

I am in a vast net-enclosed area filled with large cages.

Colossal birds observe me from each one, at least a dozen, all more than half my size. Saje is dressed entirely in brown leather with tan gloves that lace all the way up to her shoulders.

"You've found my secret hobby." Saje opens a cage and lets the bird grab on to her glove. She throws the bird out, and it flies high above us, shocking me with the span of its wings. "This one's a lammergeier, if you know your birds."

We watch the bird wing around the perimeter.

She lets out a low whistle. "Aren't they just the most miraculous creatures?"

Breathless, I follow the intelligent cruel eyes, the curved beak, the prismatic feathers. "They are beautiful. Do they belong . . . are they yours?" I ask.

"They're part of the farm, so technically they belong to Organic Provisions. But they're my babies. Other people help from time to time, but I like to be close to them, which is why I live out here some weeks."

That's when it dawns on me.

"Are we in the Gunks?"

"We are. Welcome to my home."

Saje is picking herbs and flowers from tiny pots on the kitchen counter and dropping them in hot water to steep.

"What are the birds used for?" I ask.

"Hmm. What?"

I ask again.

She looks distractedly at an ornate clock above the stove before changing the subject.

"Tell me about last night." She closes her eyes: her "listening" face, to show her mind is open and ready to receive information.

"I don't really remember what happened."

Saje attempts a grimace with her inert features. "If the doors aren't locked an hour after closing, I get an alert. I was on my way out here, so I stopped at Holistik to make sure everything was OK. That's when I found you, out cold in the lounge."

She places two mugs in front of me and leans in close, tenderly taking a fistful of the green scarf around my neck and rending off the bottom. "Matcha lace," she says, dropping the scarf fragments into the mugs. They instantly dissolve, spinning in what I recognize to be cups made with Helen's clay. "Drink up. It'll be good for your nerves."

I take a small sip, and a freshly mown lawn blooms at the back of my throat.

"I thought you'd had an episode. But you were breathing evenly. I had an emergency here, so I put you in the car and brought you with me."

"Thank you. Was I alone? When you found me?" I try to sound as innocent as possible.

"Yes. Why?"

My palms are sweating. I put the mug down before I can drop it. "I don't know."

Saje looks like she wants to ask something further, but she looks at the clock and decides against it. "I have an errand to run now, but I'll be going back to the city in a couple of hours. I can take you then."

"Thank you."

"Make yourself at home while I'm out."

"You won't be here?"

"I'll be back soon. If you get hungry, there's juice in the fridge. If you get bored, there's a lovely trail that starts right out there." She points to the side door behind me. "If you turn right, you'll end up on the farm, but if you turn left, you'll be in Witch's Hole."

"Witch's Hole?"

"State Park. You haven't been?"

I shake my head.

"Oh. Well, it's settled, then. You have to go. It'll help you meet your daily outdoor activity quota, anyway. There's a beautiful waterfall you can hike to fairly easily. Just make sure you're back in a couple hours."

Saje hurriedly deposits our mugs in the sink, signaling the end of our interaction. She opens the door for me and shows me the path. She had evidently meant that I should go on the hike right now. I gamely start the trail, feeling her encouraging glances on my back. The hem of the long white dress I am wearing is instantly sodden with mud. She must have noticed I was barefoot? The path is relatively clear, so I continue. I can't help but feel as if she's trying to get rid of me. I figure when I've been outside an appropriate amount of time, I can go back, and Saje will have left.

The house and all signs of it disappear quickly. I am surrounded by thousands of shades of green and just as many different textures of stem, twig, and bark. Underfoot, a rich tapestry of damp leaves, mostly withered and rotting in the cold. It's almost March, but there are no signs of spring. I try to remember the last time I was this immersed in a natural setting and can't think of one. The silence is so loud and persistent, it's almost unsettling. Other than my own footsteps, there is only the occasional sound of foliage brushing against me. Ferns the length of my body lick me as I pass, the tall heavy undergrowth swallowing me more with every step.

A car door slams, its echo swimming to me in concentric circles. Saje leaving. I turn around, the sound not where I expected it to materialize. Shit. I see quite clearly now that the path diverged some time ago. Without my noticing, the leaves and dirt I had been walking on had slowly disappeared. Now I am walking on smooth flat stone, laid too perfectly to be natural. I try to backtrack, but everywhere I go, there is only more dark stone—I can't find my way back.

A small wind lifts my dress and sand drifts over the tops of my feet. I keep going in the direction of the wind. Soon I am walking ankle-deep in sand.

I arrive unexpectedly at a large sandpit surrounded by the forest. It's a bizarre clearing, as if someone had forgotten to finish setting up a beach volleyball court. In the sand, a dozen or so wells have been half completed. *What are you?* A susurrus from the deep belly of the forest stirs where I imagine a conductor is poised with a baton. The wind carries with it a putrid scent, coming from the uncovered pits. I walk toward them to see what is producing such an offensive odor.

On the left, the wells are filled with swollen festering lumps gelled together. On the right, they appear to hold the same contents that have been left to dry for longer in the unsparing sunlight. The jelly substance has evaporated, leaving the rot to chalk and crumble into a texture not unlike the sand beneath my feet. I can't guess what it is, much less why it is here. Some previously farmed thing, fomented and forgotten?

A tearing noise makes me look up. An enormous male deer is watching me. He is soon joined by four, then five, others. They stand in a straight line. I back away, in case I am frightening them. They advance toward me as I retreat. I take another step backward. They take a step forward. We continue like this for a few steps, them taking a synchronized step forward for each step I take backward. There is no sound around me. Even the wind has died.

This is ridiculous. They're deer. They don't eat meat, least of all humans. I tell myself to get a grip. I exhale slowly and count to three. On three, I turn my back to them and walk in what I think is the direction of the house. A scream rises in the back of my throat when a deer swiftly appears to my left. I must be losing my mind. But surely there is something threatening in the way he looks at me and points his antlers. I turn and walk in the opposite direction.

The nature is less beautiful to me now. I keep tripping in my too-long dress, and the heavy sleeves are catching on everything. The stones underfoot have disappeared, and I'm back on a trail of sorts. I start to walk faster, cutting my feet on the sharp gravel and the cruel curled edges of dry leaves. Worried I am getting more lost. Behind me, the deer keep advancing. I suddenly see the house and break into a run, hoping the door isn't locked and that the deer won't also begin to run. I sigh audibly with relief once inside, slamming the door shut behind me and catching my breath. I look out to see if the deer are still watching me. Not only are they watching, they also seem to be waiting. One of them hunches at the neck and gives the appearance of eating something. Appearance, because there is nothing at mouth level. It opens a dainty jaw and chews on air.

My first instinct is to run to the bedroom where I woke up. I can't see any deer from the windows, but the fact that there are windows at all makes me apprehensive. Chills spider down my neck when I remember the deer trying to walk through glass. It is suddenly imperative that I find a room without windows. I look to the rooms upstairs. No deer can possibly look in at that height. I stop on the staircase, wondering if I'm trespassing.

Make yourself at home, Saje had said.

The first room I encounter must be a sort of dressing room. Gigantic wooden built-ins are lined with shoes and hangers draped with all kinds of material. There are chests with open drawers, too stuffed with clothing to properly close. Beautiful, expensive clothing for the most part, but there are also unlikely items. Camouflage jackets, industrial-looking coveralls, and muddy steel-toed boots. A perfectly round bed is centered in the next room. Silvery gray branches draped with moss gently climb in through open arched windows. Everything is a calm shade of pale green framed with dark wood, an extension of the view outside. To the right of the bed, a bathroom covered in moody black tile with a spectacular view of the mountains from a raised bathtub. The next room is basically a walk-in medicine cabinet. Entirely covered in mirrors and a veritable altar to Holistik beauty products. No windows, but not exactly peaceful either. With nowhere to escape my reflection, I see more clearly how I have changed. My calves stretch impossibly long, as does my once round face, and my dark brown eyes now gleam with algal blues and greens.

The last room is the smallest by far. Barren except for a huge desk and chair. On the desk, what must be a surveillance system. Multiple screens with cameras jumping to and from different areas. Most of the screens show trees, crops, general wilderness. I sit in the chair and relax. No windows here. The cat has followed me into this room, mewling as it sits next to me. I reach down and scratch the area underneath its neck. A car is pulling up on the most central screen. The angle of the camera flits from one side to another. Before it jumps to another shot, I see Saje in the driver's seat pushing oversized sunglasses onto her head.

The screen abruptly moves to a view of tall mountains, craggy and majestic. The view is framed by voluminous black leaves, brushes inscribing the sky. It jumps again to a man's legs emerging from another car. Or the same car. Another jump and I realize I'm on the mountain I had just seen. A mirror like the one in the bedroom downstairs is next to the video source. The cat leaps onto the desk, its paws hitting buttons on a keyboard. The giant mirror on the screen starts moving. I grab the cat from the desk and the mirror instantly stops turning.

Saje appears abruptly in frame, frowning up at the dome. She has an object in her hand. She aims it at the dome, and it begins to rotate again. Henry appears behind her. He is sweating, lugging something heavy behind him. Back to the view of the tall mountains. The branches gesticulating in the wind. This time, though, I can see a tiny Saje and Henry. The massive mirror, which I now realize is a powerful lens, is still moving. Rotating downward. It paints a pale strip of sun on a lower cliff. The light seems to intensify on that spot, gathering in high concentration.

A bird lands on the cliff. And another. Even from a distance, they are remarkable in size. I notice there are other domes, at various heights, perched on other cliffs. They all begin to move, mechanized to angle themselves toward the same area. More birds swoop down to land near the pooled sunlight. A bundle of some kind flashes on the screen. Being dragged by Henry. It looks to be made of a stiff material. Canvas? Burlap? I watch it bump and shimmy to the center of the cliff. An edge unfurls and coppery threads spill out.

The camera shifts once more. The odd glass structure. A close-up of the birds. So close I can see their individual feathers. I keep waiting. I have to see it again, to be certain. The other screens flicker through the rooms in the house. I even see myself, pale and miniature in front of the computer. The main screen displays the dark violet mountains again. I am entranced by the way the sunlight is collecting on the exposed cliff. Now turned on its side, the mirrored dome continues to function as a beam that gathers sunlight and condenses it over a specific place.

"Hello?" Saje asks.

I panic at the sound of her voice, which is tinged with disapproval. I was so enthralled by what I was seeing, I didn't notice the absence of Saje and Henry on the main screen. A small monitor on my left shows Saje with one foot on the stairs, a hand curled around the banister. What was I thinking? I should not be in this room.

"I know you're up here," she says, beginning to walk upstairs.

I try to leave everything the way I found it, turning the chair back to face the desk and positioning the keyboard the way it was before the cat moved it. *The cat!* It yowls as I grab it on my way out of the room, running and hoping I can make it to the next one in time.

"There you are! This is my favorite room in the house, too," Saje says, walking in to find me in her product room. "Find anything interesting?"

My eyes, in the mirror, are wide with panic, and sweat beads my hairline. Her reflection smiles at mine as she cups my chin with a cold hand. "Ready to go?"

"I'm actually glad we have this time to chat," Saje says once we are in her car.

I shift in my seat, trying to find a place where the wind doesn't hit me too directly. My phone overheats in my lap as it siphons power from Saje's car.

"I've been meaning to ask about your name."

"My name?"

"What does it mean?"

"It's the name of a flower. Lotus."

"It is so beautiful." Saje beams at me through her sunglasses.

It unnerves me how little she looks at the road while driving.

"I've been thinking. Maybe we can give you a different name for when you're at Holistik."

I look at her with confusion. "You want to change my name?"

"No, of course not. Just for the store."

I smile and look ahead, unsure of what to say.

She drops her voice. "Truthfully, and it hurts me to bring this up, we've had some complaints from customers. It's difficult for them. It's no one's fault that your name is in a more advanced language than the one they know. But it can make them feel excluded in a way that doesn't help with our transactional goals at Holistik. Sometimes the barrier to a great sale is simply not knowing how to address someone for a question. Besides, you would be joining the other girls."

"The other girls?"

"Madison was, I think, Jiafang. And Emerson was Lucia, and Tanner was Ha-yoon. Tanner had so much trouble deciding which sister from *Full House* she wanted to share a name with, she eventually just chose the last name!"

Saje laughs her throaty laugh while I choke back my shock. Are Madison and Tanner also Asian American? They're blond.

Naturally so, I had assumed, and blue-eyed. I think back to the times I had overheard them talking about their extensive travels to Asia. They weren't, as I had thought, white girls who ate, prayed, and loved their way to gratitude by visiting poorer countries for perspective—they were going home.

"Can I think about it?"

"Absolutely. Just let Lilith or me know by next week." She takes both of her hands off the wheel to dig around her purse. "Do you mind?"

I shake my head, surprised to see her taking out cigarettes.

She notices my reaction. "Damiana and mugwort, of course! Never tobacco." The car fills with a sweet medicinal scent as she exhales. "Remind me where you're from?"

"New Jersey. My parents immigrated from China."

"How nice! What made them want to come to America?"

My mind tries to distill the violent class struggle of the Cultural Revolution into a single-sentence answer.

"They love American food," I say instead.

Saje smiles knowingly as if she had predicted the allure of greasy burgers and creamy shakes to be too great for my immigrant parents to ignore. "And what do they do now?"

"Oh. Well, they used to be piano teachers." I pause, not knowing how much of the truth I should share. I decide to be candid. "They were actually in a severe car accident a few years ago. Now they're both in a total assistance facility."

"How awful. I'm so sorry." Behind her large sunglasses, I see that tears have formed in her eyes. She takes a deep drag from her cigarette before speaking again. "I suppose there's no delicate way of asking this, but how functional are they?"

"They've been getting better in the last few months. The doctors are hopeful about their recovery in the long-term. It's hard, though. For the most part, they still don't even know when I'm there." I surprise myself by starting to cry.

Saje reaches over and pats my left thigh a few times. "You poor thing. I'm sure they'll recover. Applebaum is a wonderful place."

We drive the rest of the way in silence. It doesn't feel like a good time to ask about the wells in the sand. I certainly don't think I should mention the windowless room I found and what I thought I saw there. *People have been let go for getting too curious*, Lilith had said. An image of a beak pulling and snapping a long spilling strand erupts in my mind. Instead, I try to remember if I've ever mentioned the name of my parents' care facility to her. I finger the mandala at the base of my throat.

"Thank you so much for the ride, Saje."

"Anytime. I'm just so glad you're OK."

Saturday is always an especially busy day at Holistik. With so many people in the store, I feel safe going downstairs to look for any signs of what happened last night.

The floor is clean where I vomited, and the Zoo door is shut and locked. There is no indication that anything out of the ordinary happened. I look at the cameras in the corners, wondering what they would reveal.

Madison comes out from the bathroom, wiping her hands on a pleated silk skirt. Her hair is the color of untouched sand on a private beach. "Hey, what are you doing here? You don't work today!"

I look at her with renewed interest, trying to make out Asian features.

"What?" she snaps aggressively.

"Sorry, I just . . . Saje told me your real name."

"My real name?"

"Jiafang."

She scoffs. "That hasn't been my name for years. I had it changed legally when I started working here."

"But are you—" I struggle with how to ask her what I want to ask.

"Are you seriously going to ask where I'm 'really from' or something?"

"Sorry, I was just surprised."

"Don't be so unimaginative. This is America. And not just America, but New York, and Holistik. I can be whoever I want to be."

"Of course." I don't know why I was surprised. Holistik has changed everything. Natural beauty doesn't exist here—it's created. Why not ethnicity?

"You can, too," she says more gently. "Are you interested in changing your name? You've always looked like a Courtney to me."

I back away slightly. "I'll think about it. I'm here to pick up some stuff," I tell her.

Her exaggerated lips pout. "You left the spa a mess last night. I had to muck out the dried dirt because you didn't rinse it off. You, like, owe me."

"I'm sorry. There was an incident."

But she's already walking away with a huff and a flip of her white-blond hair.

I go back upstairs, not sure what to do. I am only at the store because Saje had assumed I was working, and I hadn't wanted to correct her.

My phone rings.

"Hello?"

"Hey, it's Helen! Did you get my message? Do you want to meet us?"

CHAPTER FOURTEEN

Probably a hundred girls in various states of undress are crammed in the basement damp with humidity. Celery silk tulle and apricot velvet tangle with their white contorting limbs. It looks like a scene from one of Degas's lesser-known works depicting brothel workers instead of ballerinas. I walk among the sweat stains and a claustrophobic amount of fabric, searching for Helen and Lilith. There is a total lack of personal space as chipped nails and wet clammy skin grope me on the way to their desired items. I find them eventually by the gold of Helen's hair.

"Hey!" she shouts over the din, trying to wave with one arm stuck halfway through a dress hole. As she struggles to free herself from the garment, Lilith and I gasp at the sight of a nasty yellow-black bruise between her shoulder blades.

"What happened?" I ask.

Helen arches her back in the mirror.

"Oh, probably just a fall. I took a bad tumble the other day," she says quietly, rushing to put her own shirt back on.

Lilith's lips are a tight line of disapproval as she stares at

Helen's now hidden bruise. She is wearing a light gray leather jacket, so polished it looks as if she's donning a slick of oil.

"Your jacket is beautiful," I say.

"It's shark fin," Lilith says with distaste. "Another unethical gift from Uncle Victor."

"You're the one wearing it," Helen says before turning to me. "Hi."

In the dirty mirror that runs the length of a wall, I watch as Helen's reflection hugs mine. My skin has paled and my cheeks ripened. I am still depths below her in beauty, but I am astonished to see that the difference isn't as acute as I would have expected.

I follow Helen and Lilith to a half dozen other shops. I'm thankful the others aren't as overwhelming as the sample sale, but the scrutiny of small boutiques is equally intimidating. The final store they want to go to is that of a famous luxury brand.

"Are you going to get it?" Lilith's purchases are being packed up and she has wandered over to where I am running my hands over the finest material I have ever touched. The speakers in the store play the slow movement of Beethoven's Piano Concerto no. 3, and I fantasize for a moment of playing along on leather-coated piano keys.

"Oh no."

"Really? It's the only thing you've shown any interest in today."

One year during Christmastime, Ba had come home with a counterfeit bag meant to closely resemble the one I'm now holding. All his teaching wages for a couple of months had gone into the fake made of cheap pleather and brass, and my mom was wildly upset at his irresponsibility. Still, the expression on her face when she put it over her shoulder is one I will remember forever. I had never seen her look in the mirror or at anything we owned with something akin to pride. The bag was a signifier of belonging. As if having the right purse could fix what was wrong about the world's perception of Ma. Though it was barely passable as a reproduction, she carried it on every special occasion.

"Since you're not getting it, do you mind if I do?" Lilith asks as she yanks it from the display and runs to the counter.

Anything they remotely like, they buy. Sunglasses they don't need, coats for weather they are unlikely to encounter, shoes that weren't designed with mobility in mind. We arrive at my favorite part of the Beethoven concerto: scales rise steadily, only to lose confidence and falter each time until the last one, which is brave enough to continue. I stand in place, listening to the piece, and look around the store to see if anyone else has stopped to pay attention. Everyone else is more or less consumed by their pursuit of the perfect accessory. I forget that classical music is often stripped of its power in places like this, where it is used as a pacifier for the rich. If I had not been raised to play piano, I wonder if I would have ever heard one in my life.

After the shopping, we stop by a pizza place. We squeeze into a cramped booth with all our bags and let grease drip down our elbows. It is a little incongruous to see Lilith eating a slice the size of her face, but to see Helen taking big gulps of cheesy bread is surreal. I have a sneaking suspicion there's a camera crew somewhere, ready to film a commercial for the cheap flavorless beer we are having too much of. Even the neon lights seemed to dim when we first walked in, conceding to Helen's radiance.

"If Saje could only see us now," Lilith snorts through a mouthful of sausage.

Helen and Lilith laugh.

"I have a feeling your auras are going to be really heavy for tomorrow's weigh-in," Helen says.

Lilith rolls her eyes. "Imogen is so full of shit. At least she doesn't dare touch me anymore."

"What happened?" I ask Lilith.

"I seduced her," Lilith says with a shrug. "This was early on, before we knew about lanolin. I got her to kiss me, and one thing led to another until she was strapped to her own chair. Made Saje come see just how suggestible Immy's empathy actually is."

"And?"

"And nothing. Saje was disappointed in me for my 'aggression,' but eventually blamed it on the lunar phase. I mean, she couldn't really fire me. Not with how close I am to Victor and Helen."

And they certainly are close. All afternoon I had listened to them telling and retelling their favorite stories. This time, that trip, those days. They had shopped in Mallorca, ridden donkeys in Morocco, and collected sea glass in Maine, all while I sat in front of a piano. I start to understand how closely knit their lives have always been. Their childhoods take on a mythical quality. Maybe youth, I think to myself, is also something only the privileged can afford. I play a game of trying to photoshop myself into their memories, but even in my make-believe, something is off: I don't have the correct shoes, or I can't get my hair to lie right.

"Isn't it illegal to fin sharks?" I ask, interrupting yet another reminiscence (this one in Amsterdam, involving stolen bikes and a secret rave in the Rijksmuseum when they were teenagers). "I just mean, how did Victor get a jacket made of shark fin?"

"Knowing him, he probably rescued some sharks and had it made after they died. His usual zero-waste thing," Helen says.

Lilith's expression sours, twisting perversely in the shadowy light. "Or he's frequenting illegal wildlife markets."

The air between them is tense. Helen has a pained expression on her face when she asks, "Why do you always assume the worst?"

I try to make a joke. Something about making soup out of Lilith's jacket. It's a terrible joke and at my expense, but it does the trick of mostly clearing the air.

We eat our pizza silently for a while. Lilith's new quilted bag already has a light tomato stain on it. She wipes her mouth with a napkin and stares at me.

"Should we take her to the Cloisters?" Lilith asks.

"Who's the new girl?" The man is looking me up and down.

"She's with us. She's cool," Helen says.

And for the first time in my life, I feel cool. He salutes Helen and points to the door, flashing a smile at me. Every tooth of his has been replaced with wood. No, with tiger's-eye gemstones. Something flickers behind him. Lilith is already pulling the door open, giddy with excitement. I look back at the man, wondering if I have seen correctly. We walk down a long hallway. At the end of it, I see flashing lights and hear loud pumping music. The stone around us reverberates, and the walls on the left are lined with floor-to-ceiling stained glass windows. I stop in front of a pane where Jesus is pouring water onto a kneeling disciple. His

face is in an expression of contorted ecstasy as his follower seems
to earn his baptism.

"What is this place?"

Helen and Lilith grin, looking back to see my expression as
we enter. Men, seemingly built from the same stone as the walls
around us, swing from the ceiling, swallow fire, and gyrate on
platforms around us. Lilith takes a silver tin out of her pocket and
opens it, revealing a clear gloss. She takes a swipe and unzips her
pants, thrusting a hand in.

"Want some?"

Helen nods, her body oscillating to the rhythm of the music.
I look around to see if anyone is watching Lilith, but what she's
doing is comparatively tame to everything happening around us.
Helen takes a dab on her pinky, and it disappears under her shirt.
Lilith holds the tin up and looks at me.

"Yes?" she asks, and before I know it, her hand is in my pants.
With her finger, she strokes the length of me twice before slipping
inside. When I open my eyes, she's already dancing away. I am
rooted in place, first out of shock, then out of fear. I watch as
Lilith and Helen float among the statuesque men, who dance
with them. The floor recedes, and soon there is no barrier between me and the music. A man with a thong made of sparkly
streamers dances in front of me for an eternity. I hear giggling
and realize I'm the one laughing. He's tickling me with the feathers coming out from under his nails.

"Let's go! Move!" Lilith is yelling at me, urgently.

Colors swirl around her head, dazzling me. I try to move and
step on a carpet of Helen's hair. She is being dragged by someone.
It's the bouncer from earlier, with a lengthy foxtail peeking out
from under his coat.

We are sitting on a curb outside when I land in my body and come to myself again. It has started snowing lightly, and each flake on my cheek brings me back to the present.

"Welcome back, champ." Lilith is laughing, looking at my face.

Helen is holding a bag of ice to her head.

"What happened?" I ask.

She looks embarrassed. "I kind of blacked out."

"Are you OK?"

"I'm fine. It happens."

Lilith is angry. "You need to get this checked out. You shouldn't be passing out all the time."

"It's not all the time," Helen says wearily.

"Does it have to be all the time before you'll take this seriously? What happened just now was scary. So is your frequent chest pain. Why won't you just see someone? Is it Victor's bullshit? You don't have to commit to anything, just get a doctor's opinion!"

Helen sighs, readjusting the bag. "I'll think about it," she says quietly.

I rub my head and move my feet, making sure I have regained control of them. "I think I blacked out, too."

Lilith snorts, and even Helen chuckles weakly. "No, sweetie, you were high as a kite."

I remember something. "I think I was stamping my feet and neighing like a horse." I am frightened by the memory, but I laugh with them anyway.

We walk to the subway station together, tripping lightly in the fresh snow with a gratified tiredness.

"What was that place?" I ask.

"You've never been clubbing?" Helen asks, astonished.

"Not like that," I say, thinking of the clubs I had performed in as a student. Places like the Century Association and the Metropolitan Club. They had nothing in common with what I had just experienced. "It was mostly men?"

"It used to be a church, but now it's a gay club," Helen explains as Lilith shakes her head at my ignorance.

"They don't mind that we aren't men?"

"I don't think so. I hope not! Many of them don't identify as men anyway, or even mammals, for that matter. We know most of them. Almost everyone who was there tonight is a customer at Genysis. With a *Y*."

"Genysis."

"It's one of Victor's subsidiaries, focusing on genetic modifications."

I recall the tail I thought I'd imagined.

Lilith snorts. "Did you see Kyle?"

Helen shakes her head sadly.

"Guess he decided to get the integumentary sensory organs on his face, too. He says he doesn't regret it, but I think he does." She looks over at me. "This guy we know. Crocodile bumps, all over."

I shudder. "Was it a topical surgery?" I blink away the image of a doctor sewing raised bumps of skin onto a human face.

"No, they probably went in and altered the cells to get them to grow a certain way. Most likely, they used a localized virus and stopped the breeding when he was happy with how it looked. I'm sure it was so painful—post-birth gene edits are never fun. At least he's looking more like a crocodile now. For a while there he was just lumpy and kind of avocado-y."

"Victor funds that kind of stuff?"

"Victor's smart. He knows where there's culture, there's counterculture. Every established beauty norm has an equal and opposite reaction, right? He may not agree with other definitions of beauty, but he certainly wants to profit from them."

Helen sighs.

"Am I wrong, though?" Lilith fixes her with a steely glare.

"You make him sound so . . . evil."

"Not at all. I respect his hustle. Besides, he makes himself sound evil. Unironically collecting Aleister Crowley memorabilia? Be more of a stereotype."

"Those are gifts!"

"Yeah, from his weird-ass magician friends."

"He doesn't believe in any of that stuff."

"He exploits their beliefs, which is arguably worse."

"Exploits them how?" I can't help but ask.

"He experiments on them."

"Like, without their knowledge?"

"No, no. They want more than anything to be experimented on."

"So it's symbiotic," I say.

Lilith looks at me coldly. "Doesn't mean it's ethical."

Helen smacks her head with the bag of ice in frustration.

"Wow, we're here already," I exclaim, gesturing limply at the subway station.

I have a long commute ahead of me, but I'm looking forward to the time and space alone, where I can replay the day ad nauseam.

They blink up at me from halfway down the steps once they realize I haven't followed them.

"I need to transfer to the R, so I'll see you later," I explain.

"What? You can't walk there alone! Where do you live?"

"Sunset Park."

"In Brooklyn? Why don't you come over and stay the night? It's way too late to be walking around at this hour." Helen touches my arm out of concern and a need for balance. "Come on, Lilith will come, too, won't you?"

On the platform, a young man in jeans and a green pullover keeps glancing over at us, probably unable to tear his eyes from Helen. He slowly begins to approach us. I don't recognize him until he is already hovering between Lilith and Helen. It takes them a few minutes to register his presence.

"Hey . . ." I begin weakly in his direction.

He stares at me, open-mouthed in surprise. "It *is* you! You look so different; I almost didn't recognize you!"

Lilith and Helen eye him with drunken curiosity.

"This is Conor Hearst. We went to school together." I gesture at Lilith and Helen. "Lilith and I work together, and Helen is . . . a mutual friend."

They smile politely at each other. A girl is calling his name. A girlfriend, perhaps. She sounds upset, looking at us with the distrust women reserve for other women. Conor is still staring at me.

"We should catch up sometime. It's been too long."

"Sure," I say, certain it will never happen.

"Let me get your number," he says, a phone screen lighting up his face.

I recite it dumbly for him.

"Cool," he says, grinning at me. "I can't believe it's really you."

With a last look, Conor walks off, the girl pulling him with her hand. When they have disappeared from my field of vision, I wonder if I imagined the whole thing. The Conservatory and

Conor, Professor Zsaborsky and even the piano—it all feels like it happened to a different person.

Saturday night. It is crowded on the train. We squeeze together, trying to angle our bodies in the least offensive way to everyone around us. It is too loud to talk, so we smile tiredly at each other. Helen drifts in and out of sleep next to me. We are so close I can feel the heat of her breath on my cheek. Her hair smells like orange blossoms warmed in honey. The turbulence pushes and pulls us. Lilith is somewhere to the left, out of sight. Every time Helen and I are pressed together, I linger, unsticking at the last possible second.

"Who was that guy?" Helen asks when we exit the train. She rubs her eyes with both hands like a child.

"We went to school together."

"Yeah, we know that part," Lilith huffs.

"He was at the Conservatory with me. We had the same piano teacher."

"He's really hot. Did you guys date?" she asks.

"No. We slept together a few times, though," I admit.

"I knew it. He's definitely still interested in you."

My laugh echoes into the empty street. "He wasn't even interested in me then. We just have a lot of history. We basically grew up together, eight years with the same teacher in the same school . . . What you're sensing, it's probably that."

Lilith doesn't look convinced. "You slept together multiple times."

"Conor slept with everyone. He's a great pianist, and a lot of people were drawn to his talent," I say. It was unfortunate that my skill had inspired the opposite effect.

Helen's room is a light lilac color and larger than any room I've seen in New York. There is a king-size bed, an architect's desk being used for building tracing and oil painting, and flowers drying on every surface. Lilith and Helen immediately jump on the bed, waking an adorably disheveled and now disgruntled Goose, but I look around. Even though I come over regularly, I've only ever slept in the guest room. I relish the opportunity now to be in Helen's personal space.

On a desk, there are pictures of Helen and Henry together. On skis in Switzerland, on horseback in Wyoming. They don't look too similar now, but when they were young, it would have been difficult to tell them apart. Books are scattered everywhere, mostly publications on art and design. On the bed, a stuffed horse, worn with love, makes my heart thump wildly. I try not to stare as Helen stretches her arms and legs, alabaster being pulled. I look instead at her back wall, which is almost a replica of the one at Holistik, similarly full of ceramic products, but these are much larger and slightly off.

Helen notices my gaze. "Do you need anything?"

I shake my head.

"Are you sure? You know I get it all from the Gunks. There's definitely no shortage there. If you ever need a refill or want to try anything new, help yourself."

I think of how fast my own products dwindle with Alice doggedly finding each new hiding place.

"Thanks. I might take you up on that. My roommates like to get into all my stuff, so it goes pretty fast."

"These are the roommates who fucked up your eye?" Lilith asks.

"Yeah."

She frowns to herself. "How did you find them?"

"The internet."

"And they're not serial killers?"

"I don't think so. Just violent so far," I joke.

I let my fingertips trail on the giant vessels in the half-dark. "These shapes. They're so expressive."

"The ones we make for Holistik have to be uniform, but I get to exercise my creative freedom for the Gunks vessels."

"I wish everything in-store came in these sizes," I say. "I guess I wouldn't have the storage space, but still, it'd be nice to not have to lug everything back and forth for refills every two weeks. Who are the Gunks supplements for?" I ask.

"For the staff out there, the farmers and their kids, the other ceramicists, artists-in-residence . . ."

"And everyone gets personalized supplements?"

"For the Gunks staff, it's a little more general, I think. It does the job, though."

"That's—" I suck air in abruptly. The jar in my hand is covered in curved spines, razor-sharp, and one of them has sliced the inside of my left index finger, drawing blood. I put the vessel back and join them on the bed to nurse my finger.

"You're bleeding," Lilith says, taking my hand.

A trickle of blood drips down the inside of my wrist, and she catches it with her tongue, licking all the way up the stream of my arm until she reaches the cut and starts to suck on it. With her other hand, she strokes my knee.

"What are you thinking about?" she asks.

"Nothing." I make my face as blank as possible.

Lilith continues to stroke me, now massaging my inner thigh.

"Lilith, stop. You're making her uncomfortable." Helen nudges Lilith with her foot.

"You're not uncomfortable, are you? Sorry about earlier, by the way. If that was startling. Vaginal administration bypasses the first cycle of rapid metabolism."

"What was that stuff?"

"One of the guys at the club slipped it to me a few months ago. Crocodile Kyle," Lilith says, grimacing. "He swiped it off one of the witches." She laughs at my expression. "You're so gullible. Witches are what they call Victor's scientists at Genysis. It's good, isn't it? Makes you loose. More susceptible to fun." She pinches my thigh hard, smiling. "You're usually so uptight."

I press a hand to where she has just pinched.

Her green eyes glint with humor. "Hel, you should have seen her on the subway earlier. She wants to fuck you."

I can feel myself burning up.

"Am I right?" Lilith smirks at me. "She's in love, she's in love," she chants in a horrible singsong voice.

Helen groans. "You're so mean when you're drunk, leave her alone."

"I'm not drunk, I just want to know if I'm right." Her pale lips are lined in the bright red of my blood. She starts edging her fingers higher. "Don't be shy. It's perfectly normal. Everyone either wants to be Helen or to be with her. Which is it for you?"

I move off the bed quickly, out of Lilith's reach. I can feel myself pooling the thin fabric between my legs.

"OK, I guess I am a little bit drunk," Lilith says, laughing.

"It's late, I should get home," I say.

Helen sits up. "She's being an asshole. Just stay in the guest room for the night? It's too late to go home. I wouldn't even trust a car to get you there at this hour. Please."

I look from Helen to Lilith, confused. Helen is still smiling at me. I get up slowly and gather my things. I look back once, at the door, still perplexed. I can't tell if this is a game, a test, or an invitation. I fumble with the doorknob, and Lilith starts talking loudly, dismissing me.

I take my time walking down the stairs, my cheeks flush with humiliation. In the past four months, Helen has become my closest friend. Whether there is something more, I've never asked myself.

The fresh shame brings back another memory. One of the only piano performances I ever gave that could be considered a failure. A talented violinist needed a pianist for her recital. We worked together for a month on Beethoven's Violin Sonata no. 10. The first time we read through the slow movement, I was so moved by the interplay between our parts, I started crying. Thankfully she had her back toward me. During the recital, I had the distinct feeling that my hands were touching her instead of the keys. My fingers were tiptoeing across her skin, notching each rib through the soft material of her gown. I started shaking so badly I played wrong notes. The next semester, she chose another collaborative partner.

Downstairs, it's dark, and when I turn the light on in the guest room, I'm surprised to see Henry in the kitchen.

"Hey."

His shoes are covered in swampy green sediment and his suit is wrinkled. He looks extremely tired and maybe drunk. He lunges toward me in the semidarkness and a sweltering odor surrounds me.

A moment later, I find myself walking up the stairs behind him.

In his bedroom, he whirls me around, touching my breasts through my shirt. I can feel that under his pants, he is already hard. We undress, and I take him into my hands, the skin like velvet on a deer's antler. I put him in my mouth, tasting and biting urgently. He pushes me away roughly and falls on his knees to lick between my legs. I shudder. This is new, and intensely pleasurable. A vase of peonies rests on a side table, and as I look at them, their stamens seem to dilate. I feel as if they are blooming between my thighs. I hear footsteps in the hall, a faint stirring in the house. A door is shut somewhere, and then we hear the faint but unmistakable sound of pleasure. Henry enters me in that moment, sharply. I bite my tongue to keep from moaning too loudly. I remember Lilith's glittering eyes, and my thigh burns where she has pinched it. Her face is suddenly covered with a burlap sack as a large wing glides, unwelcome, into my memory. I desperately try to clear my mind, reaching for other images to replace the one that has resurfaced. I imagine Helen throwing her blond curls back, the little hairs by her ears curling with perspiration, and the many curves of her body slick, sweat dripping from her like a fresh-bitten peach. I whimper, digging into Henry's back with my nails.

"Are you close?" he groans into my hair.

"I think so."

He starts moving slower and deeper, and with each thrust I think about how Helen is on the other side of the wall, listening. I feel an unbearable heat, miasmic, rising and expanding in my body, radiating outward as I come.

CHAPTER FIFTEEN

wake to sunlight spilling into the room. Henry is still asleep, lightly snoring next to me. A smattering of stubble on his upper lip makes him look unexpectedly young. I get out of bed and quietly leave the room. A bright square of light falls in the hallway from Helen's open doorway. I listen for a few seconds before looking in. No one is there, not even Goose. The bed is perfectly made, and everything is tidy. On the nightstands there are mugs full of sediment. They must have had their morning tonics recently.

In the daylight, I notice things I missed the night before. There are sketches everywhere. Tall buildings with arched windows and curved terraces. Vivid portraits of people and animals. I touch the darkest of these drawings, an octopus so finely rendered, it looks like someone blew a tangle of smoke onto a page. I stroke one of the tentacles on the cottony paper tacked to the wall. I wonder if she meant what she said last night, if she really wouldn't mind me taking some of her extra products. I grab a couple of jars, making a mental note to text her about them later. The ceramic urns are spiked, barbed, and thorned. Their shadows in the shifting sunlight are marvelously grotesque and alive.

It is early enough that I am the only one going downtown on the R train. The city looks beautiful, and I enjoy the gentle rumble of the empty subway car. In the distance, the tops of the skyscrapers are obscured by fog, and I feel equally limitless. I check my phone for anything from Helen or Lilith and notice the date.

Suddenly, I'm eight again, sitting at a table while my parents bring me a pineapple cake with a candle in it.

"My favorite!" I say, before making a wish.

"Ready for birthday gift?" Ba asks.

He hands me a binder filled with sheet music, including my favorite piece: Schumann's *Arabeske* Op. 18. I jump up and down with joy and spend the rest of the day reading through the pieces.

They had one more gift for me that night. Ma and Ba told me to close my eyes as they each took a hand and walked me out of our home. When we stopped, I waited, feeling the cool night breeze on my face.

"Now look," Ma said.

We were in a narrow space between two houses, and they had taken me there to give me a perfect view of the full moon.

I don't recognize the women at the front desk today.

"Hi, my parents are in room 326."

They look at me with polite confusion.

"Is Margot here?"

They shake their heads. A part of me is relieved to escape Margot and another potential shakedown for the amount I owe

Applebaum, but she is also the only person I have an established connection with at the facility.

"I wanted to drop off some supplements for my parents. If Margot could take a look and OK them with a doctor, I would appreciate these items being incorporated into their diet."

"We can absolutely take them," one of the women says helpfully.

I give them the jars I had taken from Helen's supply and sign in before taking the elevator to my parents' room.

Baba won't look me in the eye when I get to the room. I can never tell if he is ashamed because he remembers who I am or because he doesn't. I try to take in everything about him. The good things, like his kind eyes, tapered at the ends, and his smooth skin. The bad things, like the extra flesh hanging from his thin frame and how haggard his face has become. He hasn't been shaved in a while, and his facial hair is growing in patches that make him seem older than he is. He doesn't seem better to me, but I don't know the metrics or signs by which doctors quantify recovery. I can't believe there was a point in time when I had been so little, I couldn't see all of him at once. Now when I look at him, I see how diminished he is.

He is still wearing his old dress shoes, though the soles are threadbare. When my parents first got to Applebaum, they were given the same orthopedic footwear as the other patients. Margot said Ba refused to let go of his own shoes, holding them to his chest like a small child. My parents had often kept things beyond their usefulness. It wasn't until I was an adult that I understood this to be a symptom of how the Cultural Revolution affected them.

As a child, I thought there must have been something magical about the things they kept. Clothing that hadn't fit anyone for years, food that was already expired when we bought it, and broken appliances beyond repair. But I trusted that the items would reveal themselves to be necessary one day and it would feel so good, when the situation presented itself, to have exactly what you needed. The only time my parents ever hit me was when they perceived me to be wasteful. I remember the unfamiliar look on Ma's face when she pushed me against the wall, pinning me to look at the food I had scraped into the garbage before slapping me. It took a long time for me to understand that only people who have had nothing feel the need to keep everything.

Ma does seem to be doing better. She makes eye contact with me. Her bedside table is filled with Holistik products I have brought her in the past, collecting dust. Her desire for nice things has faded with her mind, and it depresses me to give her the jars knowing how much she would have loved them before. Gone is her need for any kind of status or belonging. I don't know if she is more liberated or lost.

I watch them for a bit, but they show no signs of noticing my presence.

The only thing that sometimes helps is to have music playing in the background when I talk to them. Somehow, the place where music is stored in their memory is untouched, a shrine that hasn't yet tarnished. Especially if the music is something they performed or taught me, I can have a whole lucid conversation with them. It makes me feel like I have parents again. I only permit myself a conversation with them like that once or twice a year. I am too afraid of abusing this and losing them forever.

I sit down on a chair between them. "It's my birthday today. Remember when you showed me the moon?"

Ba doesn't react, just keeps staring at his hands.

"Baba," I say, my voice cracking. "Guess what I heard the other day?"

I bring up a recording of Schumann's *Arabeske* on my phone and play it for him, hoping he will remember the many hours he spent teaching me the piece. He is still looking at his hands, but I can tell he's listening. Something about his body language has subtly changed. When it finishes, he lets out a little sigh. He looks up, making direct eye contact with me for the first time in months. I am overjoyed by the recognition.

"That is you playing?"

"Yes," I lie. "It's me."

When I leave their room, Margot is waiting outside. She looks at me for a few seconds with confusion. "The girls downstairs said you were here. Almost didn't recognize you. How's the new job going?"

I sigh, too tired to play games. "The salary is good. I can pay for this month on time, I just can't pay everything I owe yet."

She looks at me like she doesn't believe me, and for a moment, I see myself through her eyes. The new clothes and shoes, hair and skin vitality.

"This is all the job," I say, gesturing at my body.

"They're finally getting better. Do you understand what a miracle that is? After what they've been through? We rarely see hope in this place. I don't think I could stand it if their recovery had to be stopped at such a crucial stage . . . but if you can't pay, I don't really have a choice."

"I'm working on it. Really, I am."

"How much longer? It's been months. My job is on the line if you can't get everything squared in the next few days."

"Give me one more week. Please."

CHAPTER SIXTEEN

What are you doing here? You don't work today either!" Madison wheels around with a hand on her hip, glaring at me with accusation.

"I want to talk to Saje. Is she here?"

"Downstairs."

"Since you're here, do you want to help me with the spiders? I don't want to feed them on my own." Madison's voice is sweet and conciliatory now that she needs help.

Holistik had been touting its new orbweaver genmods for the past month, the biggest marketing push since the beginning of my time here. They are surprisingly useful. The spiders have been engineered to grow triple the number of fleecy leg hairs. These modified fibers are then dipped in their own sticky webs to be used as false lashes without the need for additional glue. It's a new favorite among the drag queens who frequent Holistik. Madison keeps yapping at me while I slowly walk downstairs, thinking of what to say to Saje. I stop in front of a mirror and collect myself, noting how my excessive lips and lashes make me look like a caricature. Madison scowls at my distracted listening and stomps away.

Saje is sitting in the dark with her back to the staircase, gazing at a computer screen.

"Saje?"

She spins around in her chair. "Darling! Are you working today? I thought we took you off weekends until you decided on a name for in-store use."

"You did. And I'm close to making a decision. I'm not here to work . . . I'm actually here to see you. I want to talk to you about something." I pick nervously at my right thumbnail.

"How can I help?" Saje asks, tapping her foot. The top buttons on her shirt are undone, and I'm surprised to see dark brown specks on her chest. I would guess they were age spots if she weren't too young to have them.

"I hate to ask." I pause, steeling myself by recalling an image of my parents. "You've already helped me so much. But is there any way I can get an advance, or a raise, or take on more shifts or—"

"You already work full-time. Overworking you wouldn't be in line with wellness, would it?"

"I guess not."

She looks at me with concern. "What's this about?"

"It's my parents. Their facility. I used all their savings for last year and I still owe—"

Saje gasps, interrupting me. A sleek white arm reaches out from under her shirt, wrapping around her neck. A baby gibbon pokes his head out.

"Have you met Gingko?"

"No, I haven't."

"From the Zoo. He lost his mother recently, leaving me with six more months of nursing duty."

"You're . . . nursing?"

She shrugs. "Of course. Common practice for centuries, especially among tribal peoples around the world. For economic, religious, and health reasons. Our own research suggests human breast milk might be better for the animals."

"I see. I guess I didn't realize . . . Did you have children recently?"

"Oh no, my children are grown. Our herbal consultant stimulates galactorrhea." She frowns as if remembering something unsavory. "There's something I've been meaning to ask you. Why don't we have a quick lunch together? I'll finish up here in a few minutes. You can wait for me upstairs." The chair squeals as she swivels back to her computer. Gingko gives me a last look before diving back into Saje's shirt. It always surprises me how human our gibbons look.

Saje finds me upstairs restocking the shelves with Living Dust. She picks up a bottle and sighs wearily.

"What a PR nightmare this was."

Holistik's Living Dust creates self-cleansing hair, conceived with the challenges of busy mothers and working women in mind. Thousands of specially cultivated mites are released into the hair, where they constantly feed on oil, dirt, and anything else that clogs the scalp's sebaceous glands. Different media outlets had a field day with the fact that we were selling, essentially, an expensive parasite. The frenzy did little to deter women from buying it; we can barely keep it on the shelves.

We go to a little diner nearby where the strong coffee is a perfect antidote to the stony expression on Saje's face across the table.

"Did you see anything interesting on your hike the other day?" Saje asks with a tight smile.

I freeze.

"You are aware of our cameras, I believe, so answer carefully." She leans forward, her crisp white shirt somehow impervious to the greasy countertop.

I shift in my sticky vinyl seat.

"What did you see?" She surveys me without blinking.

"Birds," I say nervously.

"Yes?"

It is stiflingly hot in the diner and the fluorescent lighting hurts my eyes.

"They were eating something."

I watch as she stabs a runny egg with her fork. The food, I understand, is a prop. Saje rarely eats solid food.

"You and Henry were there."

"Yes. I can't imagine how macabre it must have seemed without context, but I want you to know that for the women, it's truly a great honor for them to give their bodies in this way."

So it *had* been a human body. I clench my fists together, afraid of making any sudden movements.

"In the Shawangunks long ago, there were indigenous peoples. Most of them have joined modern civilization now, but a good number of them stayed on to work for the farm after giving us the land. We promised we would allow them to continue most of their rituals, including the sky burial you witnessed. We benefit from it, too. Whatever the birds pick clean, we find a use for. Zero-waste and all. You saw the pits, didn't you?" She reaches across her plate for one of my plump cheeks and caresses it gently. "It's my fault. I should have been clearer about the boundaries in my home. But unless you can keep what you saw between us, I will have to let you go."

My stomach drops. I think of my promise to Margot.

"Were Victor and I wrong about you?" She looks at me with such disappointment, I feel a sick need to reassure her immediately.

"No, I—" My throat catches on an imaginary clump of collagen.

She stands up abruptly. "I have to get going now, back to the farm."

I find my voice as she puts on her coat. "I won't tell anyone," I whisper.

"I'm happy to hear that. It's the right decision, given your parents' extensive needs. We've all grown very fond of you as well. It would have been a painful transition for all of us, had you chosen to leave. Now, regarding your request . . . there *is* a way for you to make additional income within the Organic Provisions family, and as a gesture of appreciation for your loyalty, we'd like to extend your employment opportunities. I'll give you a call tonight with the details."

Her teeth flash brilliantly in my direction as she exits the diner. On her plate, a long strand of red hair lies in a puddle of stiffening yolk.

Before I head home, I stop at a café and order a green tea to calm myself. I watch as the barista carefully pours steaming water over tea leaves in a mug. After so much time at Holistik, it feels blatantly wrong to put something in my body without knowing where or how it was grown, or if it's even organic. I force myself to drink, and I'm surprised at the delicious full-bodied flavor of the tea. It gives me a level of lucidity I have been missing for a long time. I look down at the leaves, which are gently unfurling, coaxed by the hot water. They look identical to the green tea leaves I often drink at Holistik but taste completely different. I feel the warmth wend all the way through my body.

Online, I read about sky burials, the funeral practice that leaves corpses exposed to the elements, mostly in Tibet, northern Australia, and India. Buddhists do it to be of use to other living things, and Zoroastrians do it because they believe the body to be impure. The Zoroastrians even built elaborate structures for excarnation, some of which included giant mirrors to hasten the bleaching and drying of bones. In India, the vulture population has heavily declined because of the use of certain lethal pharmaceuticals. Modern-day sky burials have expanded on the old Zoroastrian mirrors, using solar contractors made of Fresnel lenses in an archaic design most commonly found in old lighthouses. The wells I had seen in the sand are almost identical to an engraving I find of an old Zoroastrian ossuary pit.

I also read that indigenous people haven't populated the Shawangunk region since the late 1660s, when they were driven out by European settlers, and I can find no trace of the Esopus people ever having practiced sky burials. How can it be possible that any of the Esopus people have survived and remained after two wars in the 1600s and are now working at the Gunks farm? I don't unearth anything about their history on Esopus Island either, but read about other rites and ceremonies that take place there. An infamous occultist spent forty days and forty nights on the uninhabited island translating Chinese literature, performing sex magic, and summoning past lives. His followers gather on the island and in the surrounding area on his birthday, taking different psychoactives and performing rituals like drinking cat blood and trying to kill one another through orgasm. It turns out the Witch's Hole State Park is somewhat of an initiation spot for hundreds, if not thousands, of actual witches. My heart spasms loudly in its cage as I read about the occultist's interest in converting Hitler to his temple of Thelema and his propensity for secretly drugging dinner guests to study them under the influence. My phone dies then, and I am relieved to have an excuse to stop reading about Aleister Crowley's followers smearing diarrhea into each other's eyes.

CHAPTER SEVENTEEN

Saje had arranged for a car to pick me up. I was seized with a familiarity as soon as I entered the car, my arm pebbling with goose bumps that matched the sedan's leather interior. Like in a taxi, the front and back were separated with a thick pane of glass. I ran my fingers across the expensive leather, the feel and smell of which reminded me of the car I took all over the city with Professor Zsaborsky when the Conservatory touted me around like a show pony, to entertain our wealthiest benefactors. As the guests nibbled tiny cheeseburgers and gulped down overflowing cocktails, I would play a few of the fastest, flashiest pieces in my repertoire before retreating to a "greenroom" set aside for me—usually a small office or a spare bedroom. Occasionally, Professor Zsaborsky would bring me a plate of food. More often, he came to collect me because the guests wanted to hear more. The hosts would ask me to play their favorite songs, pieces far beneath my technical level. *I'm not a monkey*, I would think, before arranging my face into a smile and putting my hands on the keys.

The donor functions always went late into the night. I would fall asleep at some point and mercifully wake up in my own bed at the Conservatory dorms the next morning. All of the events are a blur, except one, at a four-story home with a small concert hall taking up an entire floor. They had a decent Steinway and an exceptional Bösendorfer. I grew bored in the office and snuck upstairs to explore. I could hear everyone below, their conversations and laughter getting wilder as the night went on. On the landing, I was met with three massive paintings, each a dark violet bruise spreading on canvas. The longer I looked, the more I had an inexplicable desire to walk into the paintings.

"You feel it, don't you?"

I turned around quickly, nearly slipping in my stockinged feet.

The host of the party had emerged from a room to the left and was now looking at me with an amused expression and an empty glass. His hair was shoulder-length, leaving half his face in shadow.

"I'm sorry, I was—"

"Entranced, clearly."

"I can go back downstairs. I didn't mean to intrude."

"Please stay. They're meant to be seen."

I had the peculiar impression he was rummaging through my features. I turned abruptly to face the paintings again.

"Tell me, what does it look like to you?"

Without turning to him, I told the truth. "They remind me of Beethoven's covers. The Bärenreiter editions are the same purple."

"And what does it make you feel?"

"Feel?"

"Yes, what do you feel when you see them?"

"I guess it reminds me of Beethoven, too. In one sense, it's just a canvas and music is just notes on a page, but you can engage more if you want to. Depth, perspective, different angles."

He was quiet for a moment. "Your Beethoven was magnificent tonight. I was very moved."

I sneaked a look at him, appreciating the sincerity in his eyes. "Thank you."

"The Bartók I didn't care for. I find his music vulgar and ugly."

I suddenly felt an intense dislike for this man.

"You don't share my feelings?" he asked.

I shook my head.

He tilted his head as if considering one of the paintings. "There is an early work. Have you heard his first violin concerto? No? Quite beautiful. The solo violinist begins alone, before being slowly joined by the other instruments. He wrote it for his first love, and it has all the complexity of that experience. When I think of that piece, or Schoenberg's *Verklärte Nacht*, I think it's a waste of their talents that those composers didn't continue on that same path. Given the choice, wouldn't you choose to express beauty?"

I said nothing in response. I didn't find it very interesting to practice solely beautiful music. Beauty only reaches so far. What would a Mahler symphony be without its dissonances? Not only the excruciating ones that resemble keening, but the gentle ones, too, that bruise the listener like the memory of a beloved's fingertips. At the end of the day, it was when composers tried to grasp something at the edge of beauty, or just past it, that made the most meaningful and challenging music to work on.

"You feel the paintings pulsing, don't you?" he asked.

I had assumed my uneasiness was from his presence and the general awkwardness I often felt at these events, but I realized that I did feel an odd tremulousness. The dark colors were roiling, and I felt as if invisible spores or residue were somehow transferring onto me. I don't remember what I said, some hasty goodbye before running back downstairs. I didn't know until Helen and Lilith dragged me to the Guggenheim one day for a Rothko retrospective that what I had seen were his color field paintings.

My first impression is one of exceptional warmth. Everything is light saffron and molten gold. Ceiling-high pillars of glowing salt rocks and pillowy sculptures of an unknown substance surround me. A musky raw scent permeates the air, and I almost expect to see lions yawning and stretching on the ground, which also appears to be glimmering. A petite monk-like woman stands from behind a gold abstract structure to greet me. Her light hair is shaved close, and she is barefoot, wearing only a simple straw tunic. She bows deeply.

"Welcome. My name is Moss, and I am the receptionist at Apothecare. I've been informed you go by Anna, is that correct?"

I nod.

"You will be retrieved momentarily. Feel free to take off your shoes and take a seat. We have a sustainably harvested cork silk floor embedded with rose quartz and copper. They have rebalancing and self-love properties, so you don't have to worry about the ground sapping you of energy, and our meditation cushions are made of eucalyptus foam and flaxseed fill."

She is turning to leave when I ask, "What are these?" reaching out to touch one of the pillowy sculptures.

"Beeswax candles. A fantastic local apiary in the Shawangunk Mountains provides us with beeswax and our artists-in-residence make these larger-than-life structures with them. Beeswax is a natural air purifier, and the concept of an organic art piece that erodes with time, reflecting the ephemeral experience of all living things, is the core inspiration for Apothecare and, indeed, Organic Provisions."

She pauses a moment to see if I have any more questions before going back to her desk. As her bare feet gently thwick away on the cork, I sit on the ground and take deep breaths of the warm spicy scent around me. Moss beams at me serenely from behind her station, blinking as rapidly as her fingers type.

The wall next to Moss splits open and Saje walks through it. She is wearing a simple white T-shirt and jeans. With the exception of her shoes, I have never seen her dressed so casually. I focus on her footwear because the impulse is to stare at her enormous areolas stretching through her thin white tee. The color and texture of peach fuzz, they seem to be actively dilating, and I feel my body inching involuntarily toward hers.

"Do you like them?"

I feel heat rush to my face.

"They're made of wildcrafted oyster shell and pearl, minimally processed in a remote fishing village outside of Oslo."

"Yes, they're beautiful," I say, relieved to find that she's talking about the glittery rock formations that make up her shoes.

"We'll have to see if they're not too unrestrained for our clientele, hmm? Follow me."

We step into an elevator hidden behind the opened wall. Now that I'm behind Moss, I see that she has what must be a tattoo of ants running up the length of her calf, disappearing under her straw dress.

"Thank you for meeting me so late. I thought it would be easier to show rather than tell you." Saje presses the only button in the elevator.

The doors close and we descend.

"So, you are aware Organic Provisions consists of the farm in the Shawangunks and Holistik."

I nod.

"There are many other branches, including one we call Apothecare."

"Apothecare," I repeat.

"That's right. We pay almost six figures a year for only two nights' work a week. Apothecare provides better healthcare than Holistik and extends that to employees' family. Sounds ideal for your situation, doesn't it?"

"It does."

She takes a deep breath. "Now let's talk about what we provide. Sex work has a certain connotation. My theory is that this long-standing prejudice exists because sex work has historically been a woman's profession. Apothecare offers services that are not only safe and clean, but which also provide genuine nourishment. Every aspect of Apothecare comes with consent and safety for all parties involved, and the impact is revolutionary. This isn't your normal sordid motel affair; these are transcendent sexual experiences. Enlightenment, if you will, for both our clientele and our sex workers. Physical needs and spiritual needs are deeply connected, and we've worked hard to figure out how to fulfill them simultaneously."

I stare at Saje. I remember the articles I read the day I was hired about Organic Provisions being a sex cult. I had assumed the salacious things I read were nothing more than rumor. So little of it seemed to square with my experience of the extremely sanitized Holistik.

"I know what you might be thinking, but it's all highly regulated and controlled. Everything takes place in this state-of-the-art sustainably constructed facility. We only use organic luxury products and props, and we have spa-grade amenities. I'm sure this is a lot to take in. If this isn't something you're interested in, I can take you back up and drop you off wherever you would like to go. If you are interested, however, you can start tonight. We happen to have a client in who is always in the mood for someone new."

I think of my parents glued to their beds. Apothecare's salary would be more than enough for their continued care. For only two nights a week. Maybe I could even afford a better place for them.

"I want to do it, but . . ." I have to ask. ". . . do the other girls know?"

"We usually try to keep Apothecare and Holistik separate. In your case, I'm making an exception. I know how urgent your situation is and want to do anything I can to help. You will have to sign an NDA."

I relax a little, knowing Helen and Lilith and the other Holistik girls won't know.

Saje reaches out and smooths the hair on my head. "Even if

your parents aren't capable of recognizing what you do for them, I want you to know that they are very lucky to have you as a daughter. I hope I'm never in a similar situation, of course, but if something were to happen, I can't imagine my children would make the same choices. You are remarkably unselfish."

I want to agree with her, but Saje doesn't know how they ended up in their condition.

"And I hope you can find some measure of comfort in the fact that this is my baby," she continues. "I've tried hard to build something that is ethical. Many of the girls who work at Apothecare are in similar situations as yourself. Astonishingly intelligent and talented, but held back by life's demands on them. I wanted to create options and opportunities for women, like myself, who didn't grow up with everything."

The elevator opens into total darkness. The smell of soil is so strong, I wonder if we are still inside or if we have emptied out somewhere. I follow her onto a vast beach or swallowed ballroom. White sand granules glitter underfoot like shards of shattered glass. We step onto a dim path, crossing over a body of water. Huge fallen fragments of stone form columns in the space. There is murmuring nearby, and I see bodies in the water to my right. We reach the sandy bank at the end of the narrow path. A shining black door stands there, the only thing visible. It looks like freshly poured gasoline.

One of the stretched-out bodies in the water crumples, a deformed lily, and comes to greet us. Long wet blond hair is plastered to her pale body, and she has freckles everywhere. When she is directly in front of us, I see that her eyes are abnormally black, like someone has just punctured her pupils, and a tar-colored substance is oozing into her irises. Feigning shyness, I look away from her face, and my gaze lands on her breasts. They are so spotted I have trouble finding her nipples, which look like two raisins sunk low in her chest. I imagine biting into their wrinkled skins.

"This is Astrid. She oversees Apothecare and gets all the girls settled before their appointments. If you feel uncomfortable at any point, tell her and she'll get you home. I have to drive back to the Gunks now, but you are in very capable hands. I'll give you a call tomorrow to check on you."

Saje smiles and walks back on the path over the water.

Astrid looks me up and down. "If you wouldn't mind taking a dip to cleanse? I'll grab a robe for you."

She has a faint unplaceable accent. I fumble with my clothes, self-conscious about my body and its acetic smell after a day of walking and subways and sweating. At first, I wait for her to turn away, but she never does. I shiver as the glacial water licks my ankles and then submerge myself, swimming a couple of laps before surfacing. In the water, something long congested dislodges in the back of my throat, and a rush of warmth in my chest overwhelms me. I am unsure of what is coming, but the mystery is a welcome change in a life that has been full of waiting.

Astrid is standing with a robe at the shore. I dry off and put it on, taking a few deep breaths. We walk together toward the door. My feet are heavy in the sand as she leads the way into what looks like a sunken cathedral.

"We've obviously redone everything. It was moldy and decrepit when Saje found it."

Dusty pews have been pushed to the edge of the space, and a dark rose-colored pool gleams suggestively in the center of the stone floor. Though it is out in the open, the pool has an air of privacy. Bunches of eucalyptus and black ranunculi cover every surface, imparting their wild fragrances. The walls are lined with murky stained glass windows and softly lit mirrors.

A woman and man walk up to us, removing my robe and assessing my body. I stay perfectly still while they lift and cup my swollen breasts and pinch various parts of my lower body.

"You bathed?" the woman asks.

"Yes."

At each vanity, there is a small tub. She takes the one nearest to her and unscrews the lid. Inside is a beautiful cream. Translucent, like opals ground and milked. She rubs my entire body with the substance, finishing the whole tub. I stare at my hands, marveling at the sheen. It reminds me of the hand cream provided for us by Professor Zsaborsky at the Conservatory. We always used it after lessons to heal our overworked hands. The woman helps me slip into a tight jute dress. The fabric is rough, rubbing my body in a way that excites me. She adorns my limbs with dainty chains, paints an iridescent green on my eyelids, and uses the same paint to draw long stalks of grass on my legs and fingertips.

The man takes my thick rope of half-wet hair into his hands. He shapes and pins it, finishing with a spray that smells so forcibly of mango, I start to salivate. I look in the mirror and see someone aggressively sexual. I suddenly wish that Helen could see me right now. My hair is dark again, dripping with the product he massaged in it. Black hair sweeps across one side of my face, glossy and curvaceous as a piano lid, tumbling from my neck to my waist. The man gently brushes a lurid orange gloss onto my lips with his thumb.

"You're ready," he says.

I stand on shaky legs in heels that are little more than a few bamboo stalks woven together and enter a decontamination chamber. Somewhere, air is blowing. That is the last thing I remember.

CHAPTER EIGHTEEN

wake to blood in the bed and a mouthful of sour mash. There is a heaviness to the room, and the air smells thickly of iron. It takes me a few seconds to realize I am home, in my bed. My body throbs with bell-like clarity. I desperately need water. In my room, it is so quiet I can hear my blood's slow gush on soft cotton, like the sound of mud settling after rain. I sit up and watch the red bloom between my legs, blotting out the cream of my sheets. Counting the bruises on my calves, I see that one looks like a poached egg just beneath the surface of my skin. The crimson yolk has broken, is beginning to run.

Three in the morning is early enough for me to sneak a shower in Alice and Charlie's bathroom. I tiptoe up the stairs, careful not to bloody the mildewed rugs in the hallway, and dump the cat from her nap in the sink to rinse the tang from my mouth. The cold water is sweet and has a pleasant numbing quality. I turn the shower to the hottest setting and watch my reflection disappear in the mirror as hot steam fills the room. My chin is the last thing I see, pointed like a fang. I had dripped blood on the dirty tile in the bathroom, and it is viscous, congealing before my eyes. I slip a foot under the spray, my skin reddening instantly under the heat. The bruises begin to pulse with the incessant ritualistic music of my blood. Loosened by the steam, my pores swing open, releasing a scent of jasmine and something unidentifiable, sharp like petrol. The smell blooms around me, caking the plasticky shower curtain. I reach a hand between my legs and carefully feel for the source of my pain. With my fingers, I coax the black seeds out of me. They tumble out, a couple at a time, then all at once. Gummy on the outside with an impenetrable core. I stare as they dance around the drain like pinballs before disappearing.

My phone is dead, so I leave it to charge in the basement as I brew hot coffee in the kitchen and take tiny sips from a large mug. The burning coffee helps me a little, chasing the numbness from my limbs. A scab like a thin ribbon winds around my right arm. Downstairs, I notice a white fluffy robe tossed over my folding chair. It is so pristine, it makes everything around it look soiled. The letters *O* and *P* are embossed on the left breast in a beautiful dark red script. I toss it on and sit down to scroll through my emails.

There is one from Saje with an attached contract that has my signature. There is also a copy of a nondisclosure agreement and a health form giving Organic Provisions permission for any and all health procedures they might need to perform on me. I don't remember signing anything, but I recognize my signature on every page. I try to read the contract, struggling with what seems like an unnecessary amount of legal jargon. As far as I can tell, the conditions in the contract are exactly as Saje had relayed them. It's almost more unbelievable to see everything in print. I have a direct number to a private hospital if I want any appointments made for myself or my immediate family. I am now a member of various yoga and Pilates studios, climbing gyms, and other studios for exercises I have never heard of, such as choreo-mania cardio. I have an assigned therapist with bimonthly appointments. As long as I work for them, they wire me money every month. My heart pounds as I log into my bank account. Though I know what to expect, I am still astounded.

Helen had called. So had Margot. Many times. There is a message from Margot telling me I need to get to Applebaum right away. Instead of the usual dread I have reading anything from Margot, I feel galvanized and capable. I throw some clothes on and decide to take a car, my new wealth already influencing my choices. From the backseat, I look out onto the East River and enjoy having a view of the city, space to myself, and the lack of intrusive looks. I could get used to taking cars more, the subway less. I check my bank account one more time to make sure it wasn't all a dream. The relief is immense and giddying. I try to figure out what to tell Helen. I end up with: *Hey, I'll call you back soon. I need to check on my parents at their facility.*

She texts back immediately: *What facility?*

Margot is at the front desk, and I rush to her excitedly.

"I have the money. I can pay everything that's owed right now."

Margot looks confused for a second before her face sags.

"That's not why I called."

I search her eyes for a moment. "What is it? Are they OK?"

"I'm so sorry. We've done everything we can, but they deteriorated overnight, and we don't know why. We called in a specialist."

Margot grabs me so I won't fall. My hands cover my mouth,

but sounds escape anyway. Margot leads me to a row of chairs in the hallway and helps me into one.

"But they were getting better," I protest uselessly.

"The specialist will tell us more. This could just be a little hiccup in their recovery. I need you to calm down, OK?"

I stare at her until the ringing in my ear subsides. "What are the symptoms?"

"They're not swallowing any foods or liquids, and they have tremors. Constantly."

I don't know what to say. They can't be getting worse now that I can finally care for them. "Can I see them?"

An hour passes before the specialist opens the door and lets me in. "I want to be honest with you," he says, sitting across from me in a light blue chair with the stuffing spilling over. "We've never seen anything like this. This amount of degeneration usually takes years or even decades. It's especially surprising because their records show that they had been recovering."

I nod, pinching my arm to keep from crying.

"Can you think of any change that could have caused this regression? Do you remember noticing any signs?"

I try to think clearly back to my recent visits. Did I miss something? The specialist has begun to blur, his features receding into the landscape of his face as my eyes fill with tears.

"It's possible there weren't any signs," he says gently. "But if you remember anything that might be helpful, let us know. In the meantime, we'd like to run some tests. If that's OK with you, of course. We'll need you to sign the necessary paperwork."

I nod and the tears fall.

Ma and Ba are in bed with their eyes closed as usual, but they shudder erratically. I sit between them, holding their hands when the tremors are particularly long or bad. They need to be transferred to a hospital, and I decide to stay with them.

Helen helps me pack a few things to bring with me. A toothbrush and some clothes. I am too exhausted to be embarrassed by my basement room. Too tired to fight her when she insists on coming in with me. I can see her assessing the space I live in with concern. Putting a finger to the damp wall, examining the rust on the barely working toilet.

When we go upstairs again, Alice and Charlie are having breakfast in their pajamas. They stare at Helen. The sun is coming in through the kitchen window, illuminating the dark rose undertones of her slender arms, and her hair is loose, the gold dazzling. I feel a perverse pleasure in how Alice and Charlie are looking at her. Alice is pretty, but by societal standards, Helen's beauty is unsurpassable.

"Oh my god, you're Helen Carroll," Alice says, more to herself.

Helen regards them seriously, her eyes a darker gray than I have ever seen.

"I'm such a big fan of your work . . . I saw you in *Crema* and *Aujourd'hui Jolie* and what's the other, I'm blanking now, but I can't believe—"

"Thank you," Helen cuts her off.

For the week I spend with my parents, they sleep most days and nights without any cognizance of my presence. I listen as the slow drips of their IVs count the seconds.

I sleep in a chair next to them, and in my dreams, I crawl into their minds. They had trained my fingers to find impossible sounds, and now I use those skills to find the places in their minds most in danger of disintegrating. My fingers multiply and grow long enough to become scaffolding, connecting their fragmented memories, reconstructing identities. By the end of the dream, they are so close to being fully healed that when I wake and see how little they have improved, the horror is fresh. The days are unbearably long, and I pass the time by listening to the old recordings I have of my parents.

The last time I ever heard Ba play was at the end of a small recital for his students. A local church allowed my parents to use their congregation space every so often for recitals. Their students would play for an audience of their parents and each other. On this occasion, Ma and Ba got a standing ovation from their students, a heartfelt thank-you for their dedicated teaching. The students started chanting Ba's name, wanting him to play something, too. He shrugged it off at first, embarrassed and wanting to keep the focus on the success of his students. He gave in to them eventually, sitting down to play Ryabov's *Fantasia*.

In the piece, the player is asked to strike the keys violently, almost at random, with a foot on the pedal to sustain the sound of the attack. Afterward, the pianist silently depresses a chord and releases the foot pedal. The trauma fades, and the sympathetic vibrations of the instrument allow the once silent chord to be heard. It is otherworldly, hauntingly pure and beautiful. Yet it is only heard at all because of the violence that released it.

On the last day I stay with them, a knock comes at the door.

"She said she was a friend," a nurse says from the hallway.

Helen walks in, very pale, with dark violet half-moons under her eyes. She hugs me.

"How are they?"

I shake my head.

"I would have come earlier, but I've been—" She breaks off and sighs, looking at them. "It doesn't matter. I wanted to bring you this." Helen has a long box strapped to her back. "I got you this for your birthday and thought it might be nice to have while you're here. I hope it's not offensive. If you don't feel ready, I can return it."

She takes the item from her back and places it on the floor before opening it.

I sink to the ground, overwhelmed with conflicting feelings of grief and joy, and let myself cry uncontrollably.

Helen unpacks other things she's brought for me. Soft blankets and sweaters to fight the aggressive air-conditioning of the hospital. Home-cooked meals, infinitely better than the food in the cafeteria downstairs. She brings me tea in a Styrofoam cup and stays for a while, catching me up on everything I've missed and trying to make me laugh. I introduce her to my parents as best as I can, wondering what they would have thought of our friendship.

"I'm sorry I can't stay. I have to get back to . . ." She trails off awkwardly.

"Thank you for coming at all. It means so much to me."

"Wait," she says, on her way out. Her hand is outstretched, and there is a parcel in her palm, wrapped in paper.

"What is it?" I ask.

"Something I made. In case you hated the keyboard . . ."

"Thank you," I say, feeling tears prick my eyes again. I unwrap a small sculpture—a smooth white shape twisting into black and back to white. An abstract interpretation of piano keys.

"I love it," I whisper, marveling at its intricacy.

That night, sitting on the edge of a blue hospital chair, I play again. It is difficult, even painful, to sit down in front of the keys and to force my fingers on them. When I start to feel sick or scared, I imagine Ba's fingers on the piano with mine and remember Ma's voice singing along. With their help, I am able to keep going. It is my first time playing in years, and my fingers feel the difference. It's as if they are stiff or numb from cold, but I know it is permanent. My time away from the instrument has cost me precious dexterity and mobility. The keyboard Helen brought doesn't have all the notes of a real piano, so where one piece ends, I start another, weaving Ravel's "Ondine" with Debussy's "Pagodes" and Messiaen's *Regards*. All the pieces my parents had loved and taught me. I imagine the sound of every note building on the last, fabricating a bridge by which my parents can come back to me. As I keep playing, my leaden hands lighten, running quicker and quicker. Something inside of me drops away, some fear or grief slowly untangling. When I finally stop, their ragged respiration has changed. For the first time that week, I fall asleep to the lullaby of their deep breathing.

CHAPTER NINETEEN

W e missed you!" Madison says, accosting me with a hug as soon as I step through the door. "How was your week with your parents?"

Lilith scoffs at her. "It's not like she was on vacation." I'm surprised when she hugs me, too, more gently. "We did miss you, though."

"I missed you guys, too. It was fine. I'll put my stuff away and be right up."

I hurry downstairs before they can see how much I'm feeling.

Truthfully, I had missed my coworkers. Even if our interactions aren't always warm, we are accustomed to one another. When I left the hospital last week, it was freezing outside, and as a wild gust threatened to overtake me, I realized with a sudden throb that I am almost an orphan. I don't have any other family in America. I wondered if I should call someone in China. I have family members there, but I have never met them. It had become too difficult for my aunts and uncles to see how well my parents had done in America. The distance between their lives was unbridgeable. Of course, my parents were poor by Western standards, but they had a freedom their siblings envied and resented. Talk of visiting each other ended when I was young, and eventually, communication stopped altogether. What would I say to them anyway? Chinese, which was my first language, is now a foreign one.

Lilith follows me downstairs. "How are they?"

"Not great. The doctors still can't figure out what's going on."

Lilith is silent. "Sounds familiar."

"What do you mean?"

"The doctors can't figure out what's wrong with Helen either."

"Wait, what's going on with Helen?" I almost drop the hanger in my hand.

"She finally went to get her chest pain and clumsiness checked."

"And?"

"And she started exhibiting more symptoms while she was there. She's been staying at the hospital so they can run more tests, but she was cleared to go home today."

"I can't . . . Why didn't she tell me?"

"You have a lot going on," Lilith said. "She probably didn't want to put more on your plate."

I nod quickly. I had gotten the sense Helen was keeping something from me when she visited the hospital.

"I'm going to visit her after my shift. If you don't mind waiting around, would you want to come?"

"I would love that. Thanks, Lilith."

"Oh, and I'm sorry about this, but it completely slipped my

mind to get in touch with you about your semiannual review. I should have reached out last week to make sure you could do it. You're scheduled to meet Victor during your lunch break at two."

Although the teahouse is only a few streets away, it is so nondescript that I pass it a few times before finding it, and I arrive late as a result. A beautiful tray of cast-iron pots and ceramic bowls is on the table between us. A man comes periodically to shave different herbs and flowers into porcelain cups before pouring hot water over them. Victor asks for buckwheat honey cake served with kumquat frosting. I order a bowl of cardamom-stewed apricots on a bed of amaranth. The smells and tastes are intoxicating.

"The purpose of this meeting is to make sure our ideals remain aligned going into the next year of your employment," Victor says.

I nod with a mouthful of spiced fruit.

"It may be hard to believe, but I had a difficult childhood. Sometimes I look around today and still can't believe where I am. Saje has told me that you like to walk after work, is that true?"

I nod.

"Have you ever been to the Elizabeth Street Garden?"

I shake my head.

"I had very little parental supervision growing up, and, oh, don't look so sad. Believe me, that's the way I wanted it. The alternative, my dad's attention, was not something my siblings or I desired. Anyway, I would walk around all the time as a kid, and one day I happened upon that place. I'm on the board of directors now, partly because I'm so grateful for what I learned there.

"You can imagine, I'm sure, that there wasn't much beauty at the Wald Houses, where I lived, so when I saw my first peony, it was somewhat of a shock. I could never have imagined that the bud, which looked to me like a tight fist, would develop into something so beautiful. It was a spiritual experience. Beauty gets a bad rap for being 'on the surface,' but I truly believe that it penetrates deeply into the heart of what connects us as humans. Witnessing that transformation made me believe in a similar trajectory for myself. It was the beginning of the long journey I would take to become who I am now. I went back every day to watch the peony's progress, to watch each petal spread, heavy with the weight of its own glory. In a sense, I'm still trying to emulate it today.

"Since that moment, it has become my purpose to create and preserve beauty wherever possible. That's why I connected with Holistik's mission. It was the perfect jumping-off point for Organic Provisions, and since then, we've expanded into every field. All in service of beauty."

He looks at me for a long moment. I take a sip of tea to avoid prolonged eye contact.

"You really are very beautiful. Getting more beautiful by the day, don't think it goes unnoticed. Have you decided on a new name yet?"

"Anna."

"Anna. Simple." He tilts his head. "Well, it could be simpler, I guess. Both of the letters are used twice."

"Economical," I say, offering another interpretation.

He is quiet, circling the rim of his cup with a gold-laden finger. "It feels like a lifetime ago, doesn't it?"

I wait for him to elaborate.

"The day we met."

I smile politely. In truth, I have no trouble remembering the day I stepped into Holistik for the first time. It was less than a half year ago.

"Perhaps it's on my mind because I recently gave that particular Rothko trio to a museum."

I look up at him, startled. "What?" My voice echoes in the empty restaurant.

"I know. It was difficult to part with, but it was the right decision. Everyone should be able to see it. Feel it. You remember the pulsations? That was a wonderful little recital."

"I didn't . . . You were there?"

"Of course. It was my event, as your sponsor. You must have wondered how you were able to afford all those years of tuition for free. From my understanding, you and I come from similar backgrounds."

I struggle to keep my mouth from dropping open. "I had no idea. I—thank you," I stammer.

"Of course. It was a privilege to give your remarkable gift to the world."

I knew Victor had funded the spectacular Conservatory Hall and that he was a benefactor for the school, but I never had any idea he also sponsored individual students.

The memory is coming back to me. "You had long hair."

"That's right. Helen was quite taken with your videos on the internet and showed them to me when she was young. You had so much potential. Such a strong technical player, and yet something was consistently off about your sound. I thought with the right training, that edge could be refined. Janos, or Professor

Zsaborsky, as you know him, was always a good friend, and I knew he'd be perfect for the job."

"You're not upset?"

He takes the slenderest sliver of buckwheat cake. "Why would I be upset?"

"Well, I'm no longer pursuing piano. After everything you provided."

"That depends. Do you want to be pursuing piano? What is it that you want to do with your life?"

I'm at a loss for words, unable to remember the last time I thought about what I want.

"I did. Maybe I still would, if it weren't for—" I break off before I start to cry.

I try again. "Everything has been on pause for a long time because I have to support my parents. I suppose, piano or not, I've just always wanted to make them proud. Something of an impossibility now."

Victor places his teacup gently on its saucer. "Anna, I'm sure your parents are proud of you."

I look down at my lap, stunned by how much his words make me feel.

"I understand that it may feel like a waste to you, after all those years of diligence. But the most important objective is to create beauty in the world. With piano, with art, or, in your case, with your outward appearance. There's no need for you to do anything other than to exist."

For the entire two-minute walk back to Holistik, I agree with him. Only when I'm alone again do my own thoughts come freely. He's wrong about the need for refinement in my sound.

In my early days at Holistik, Saje taught me that the trick to selling anything is to carefully maintain the balance between pleasure and pain. Customers who are fully satisfied require no further satisfaction. They must be sold a version of themselves that is constantly just out of reach. I believe in the same approach for music. Too harmonious, and everyone falls asleep. It's the sheer grip, that bit of nail, that has always made my playing what it is. That fine line between beauty and ugliness, ripeness and rot, is what keeps an audience listening with held breath.

When I get back to Holistik, Alice and Charlie are perusing the store under Tanner's watchful eye. Alice sidles up to me with a look of excitement, and Charlie follows reluctantly.

"Hey, roomie! Give us a tour!"

A smile frozen on my face, I steer them around as professionally as I can. Ever since our bizarre altercation at home, our interactions have been strained. I can't stomach being around Alice. I'm tired of her false cheer and recoil at her fragrance: a combination of the same rose perfume every girl in the city wears and the sickly sweet scent of kitty litter that permeates our shared spaces.

Alice oohs and aahs at different products, and Charlie looks as if he would be interested if he permitted himself to be. Instead of using our little pearl spoons, she dips her fingers into every tester, ruining thousands of dollars of product. I see Tanner surreptitiously throwing away the expensive testers behind us. I walk into Alice when she stops abruptly and gasps.

She starts trembling and stares at me with her eyes wide. Charlie, embarrassed, moves away from her, mumbling.

"I don't feel well!" she whispers dramatically.

I follow the store protocol. "Can I get you a tincture? Or water? Juice? I can bring you anything from the Holistik café next door."

"No! I don't feel . . . well!"

I look at her dumbly. Her eyes are peculiarly bright, and her cheeks are flushed and ruddy. She got a haircut recently. Bangs, blunt and uneven. She is dressing more like Lilith, too, copying to the best of her ability the pictures of Lilith posted online by street photographers. Though they have never met, Lilith is something of a celebrity and Alice is hardly alone in being a little bit obsessed.

"Like, the energy? In the furniture here? It's *off.* I sense *suffering.*" Her loud hissing is getting looks from other customers. Making them uneasy.

I fake a loud laugh and take her by the elbow. "Alice, let's talk about this at home, OK? I can put you in touch with Lilith if you want to talk about this with her."

"But—"

"Not now, Alice."

She waves awkwardly from outside as she and Charlie walk away, and I smile back detachedly. I loathe and envy her shamelessness.

CHAPTER TWENTY

The place smells strange when Lilith and I arrive. Takeout containers and empty bottles of alcohol litter every surface, and a crystalline silence hangs in the air. The dark wood floors reflect candlelight flickering beyond the hallway.

We slowly walk toward the light and see Helen on the floor of the living room, curled up with her back facing us. Goose is asleep, or so I think until I see the dried blood by her fuzzy ears. I place a hand lightly on her back and sigh with relief when she whimpers. Lilith and I exchange looks of confusion.

Helen is asleep with flecks of food in her hair, on her face, and on her baby blue sweater. Dark red marks streak her vomit. Lilith tries to shake her awake gently. She opens her eyes, and we notice the enlarged pupils. We sit her up, in case she needs to throw up again. She looks around without recognition and starts to cry.

"Helen, what happened?"

Her eyes roll into the back of her head before closing.

I look at Lilith in alarm. "Is she drunk? I'll call the hospital."

"No! Not the hospital," Helen says, opening her eyes again and shuddering as she speaks. Her breathing sounds like bits of metal caught in a fan. "Too late," she explains, reaching for a glass of water on the table.

I look down at my hands and see they're filled with clumps of her hair. Lilith gazes up in horror at Helen, who is guzzling water down. Her body has changed incredibly since I saw her a week ago. She is bloated, with wads of thick flesh oozing out of her pants. Her skin is covered in fine white fuzz. Her blond hair is slicked with oil, so scarce in places that her scalp is showing through. In the candlelight, we see that Helen's blond hair has been shedding on every surface of the room. I try to take the empty water glass from her.

"Stop taking everything," she spits at me.

We manage to drag her to the upstairs bathroom and clumsily try to wipe the puke off her.

Lilith looks at me in panic as Helen starts throwing up. "I'm going to call Henry. Maybe Victor. Are you OK with her?"

I nod.

"Maybe a bath?" Lilith suggests.

I run the bath and put some toothpaste on a brush, awkwardly poking her in the mouth with it. She is barely lucid, nodding off every so often. I help her get up, spit, and rinse.

She isn't just bloated. Buttery discolored skin has begun to puddle around her joints, not yet settling in. Even her feet have a layer of pudge on the top, each toe inflated, ending with a jagged broken-off nail. She focuses on me with bleary eyes.

"You have to stop."

I inhale shakily. "What?"

She laughs a little, not answering.

"Stop what?"

She doesn't say anything else, so I keep brushing her hair and checking the water temperature. I put in some soap and light a few candles. Help her out of her clothes while trying not to stare. I contemplate throwing her rancid clothes away but decide to bunch them up and toss them in the corner of the bathroom instead. She looks like a marble sculpture, so lifeless and pale in the warm water that her blue veins are visible. I find an old bottle of bubble bath liquid in the cabinet and add it to the water for soapy coverage, more for my sake than hers. I pour rose-scented shampoo into my hands and gently massage her head. She hands me her sponge and holds out an arm for me to wash, closing her eyes. I don't know whether she is asleep or awake while I thoroughly scrub every part of her body.

She sits up in the water suddenly as I put the sponge in a ceramic tray. "Stop taking everything," she growls.

"Helen, it's me." I still use my Chinese name with her. "I haven't taken anything from you."

She falls back in the water, satisfied, and reaches a pruny finger to caress my cheek. "I love you, you know." My heart stops at this admission, wishing I could be sure that she meant it.

She closes her eyes and continues babbling. I detach the showerhead to rinse her hair. I stand her up and dry her with two fluffy towels. She already seems healthier, her skin glowing from the heat of the water. Her nipples look like the soft snouts of baby pigs. I wrap her hair in a towel and help her to the bedroom. Prop up the pillows on the bed and lay her down as gently as I can.

Lilith comes in, shaking her head. "I can't get in touch with either of them."

"Please, please don't leave me," Helen says, staring at us wildly. She is shaking from head to toe.

I rub my eyes to make sure they aren't merely out of focus. My phone pings a couple of times, two audible daggers. I read the text: *Where would you like to be picked up for your service tonight?*

"Shit."

"What?"

"Nothing. I don't want to, obviously, but I have to go soon."

Lilith doesn't look at me, but she raises an eyebrow. "It's late."

"I have . . . another job. I can't afford care for my parents otherwise and—"

Lilith waves a hand at me. "You don't have to explain. I'll stay with her."

"You'll call me or text me? If she needs anything?"

"I will."

"OK. Thank you."

I get up and awkwardly kiss Helen on the forehead with Lilith watching. I cover her with the downy sheets and faded comforter, lift her arms from under the covers and wrap them over her tattered stuffed horse. Goose has made it upstairs and onto Helen's bed. She eyes me dolefully as I tuck her in, too. I walk to the door and look back at Helen. She is already snoring lightly, and a bit of drool is escaping her rosebud lips. My heart swells and I turn away before letting myself think, *I love you, too, you know.*

CHAPTER TWENTY-ONE

W e're here, Ms. Anna."

I wake confused by the name and my surroundings. Wilden helps me out of the car, and I walk down a set of stairs into the basement of an abandoned building on a quiet street. In the long hallway, I tread quickly, trying to escape the pervasive and bizarrely metallic floral scent. Moss opens the door to the golden room for me.

"Good evening, Ms. Anna. Would you like something to drink while you wait?"

"I'm OK, thank you."

I sit with my back against a beeswax pillar and text Lilith: *Everything ok?*

The warmth of the room is intoxicating, sublimating my anxiety about leaving Helen.

Astrid rushes out of the elevator. "Hi," she says breathlessly. An orchid purple robe slips off her shoulders. "How are you feeling?"

I hesitate, wondering if I should tell her I can't remember anything from the other night.

"I don't actually remember too much about that night," I say, taking a gamble.

"That fun, huh?" Astrid laughs. "Don't worry. That's not unusual. I was worried about it, too, when I first started, but Saje explained that it's normal. We experience such a high volume of pleasure that we're in a transcendent state for most of the evening. You may not remember much, but in your day-to-day, you'll start to get the sense of calm and general wellness that comes from psychosexual alignment. A lot of the women here think of their services as a kind of sexual meditation."

I nod and smile in agreement but think of the black gummy seeds I had to dig out from between my legs the following morning.

"There was some pain," I say. "And I had to remove something from down there."

Astrid nods knowingly. "Papaya seeds probably. We use them as an organic insertion alternative, among other things. I've found all sorts of crazy stuff." Her laughs sound sterile in the elevator. "The natural toys are much better for the environment in terms of production, of course, but they're also healthier for us. I can't believe I *ever* put foreign manmade materials into my body. A lot of our organic sex props have nutritional benefits when inserted regularly, too. Papaya, for instance, is antiaging."

We reach the lake, and I take my clothes off reluctantly, remembering how cold the water is. My body loosens as I swim around the perimeter. I open my eyes underwater. Activated charcoal, the cleansing agent, billows around me in arabesques of ash and shadow. I hold my hands in front of me and see only wrists, everything else hidden by the dark alluvium. The lapis columns glimmer in the dark, extending to the bottom of what is visible. When I emerge at the shore, Astrid hands me a towel and robe. The same man and woman are waiting inside the cathedral. They rub the cream all over my body, like before.

"You're all set," the woman tells me.

I look at myself in the mirror, bare-faced and naked. "No makeup or hair for me today?" A pretty, snub-nosed blonde is at the next station being draped in kelp and smothered in scales made of diamond chunks. An intergalactic mermaid in the making.

The woman shakes her head. They start to walk away, so I enter the decontamination chamber.

I can just make out the edge of the stage on my right. My body is rigid, tense under a restrictive silk dress. My fingers play in the highest register of the piano. The sound comes to me from far away, like ice clinking in a thick-cut glass. Ma is onstage, too, in a hospital bed. I part her graying hair and find the siphon there. I decant oil and pour, watching it settle as the smooth pearl of her brain starts to fizz and pucker. I knit the top of her head back together with porcelain chopsticks. She gets up from the bed with a new lightness and joins the audience. "This one is for my dad!" I tell the crowd, before I begin to play the piano keys, which are made from hundreds of pressed rose petals piled on top of each other. With each keystroke, fragrance is released along with a soft sound, like the fluttering of wings. There are thorns under some of the petals, and occasionally one threads itself into my fingers. Thin branches break through my nails, curling over the keys to play impossible chords. At the end, I stand up and take a bow. The petals are stained red and light yellow. A floral sculpture, leaking oil into glass jars. Instead of clapping, everyone in the audience leans in and takes a giant sniff.

CHAPTER TWENTY-TWO

wake with a start to Lilith calling at 4:12 a.m.

"Hello?"

Silence on the other end.

"Lilith?"

"I fell asleep," she says quietly.

I yawn and look around. I'm at home, in my bed. "I was asleep, too."

"I fell asleep. And now she's gone."

"What do you mean? Who?"

"Helen. She's gone."

"Where did she go?"

"I was in the guest room, and when I woke up, she wasn't in her room."

I sit up slowly, registering the stiffness in my limbs. A faint wail starts on the other end of the phone. I begin to worry.

"Lilith? Where are you? Are you still at Helen's?"

"I'm at Bellevue. Can you meet me?"

———————

The man who rushes me through the door wears a white lab coat with a name tag identifying him as Dr. Kenneth Sato, forensic pathologist.

I follow him to a different part of the building and shiver with cold. Lilith materializes, digging her nails so deep into me, I'm certain she has drawn blood. The doctor looks at Lilith with concern.

"I've tried to explain to her that only family members are allowed," he says.

I nod, understanding. "That's OK, we can wait here."

Dr. Sato looks at me with confusion and glances at something in his hand. Helen's driver's license.

"But surely you're family? You look just like her."

I look up at him, not comprehending.

"She's just in shock," Lilith says.

"And as a family member, you're authorizing her as a guest? I have to ask officially," Dr. Sato says.

I nod dumbly.

Dr. Sato waves us through multiple entryways by scanning the card around his neck. Finally, we stop before a pair of steel double doors. He turns and considers us. "Are you ready?"

Ready for what? My skin prickles with a thick layer of gooseflesh. Dr. Sato and Lilith go into the room, and I force my feet to follow.

Helen's dead body is laid out on a chrome slab, her flaccid skin oozing over the edges of the table. She is utterly unrecognizable. The skin on her face is so loose, it sags over her ears. Her nose is shapeless, no longer holding form. The long shapely fingers I have so often admired have consolidated, her fist a chaotic jumble of nail and skin. Her eyelashes are so long and thick, they look like needles vertically stabbed into her eyelids. In fact, they look to be growing down into and through her right eye, which is slightly open and pooling with a red and yellow liquid. She is a greenish hue, and the white fur on her body has grown many more inches. Her mouth is open, unable to close around a bloated purple tongue, pocked with white spots. A bright overhead light shows the large gaps of missing hair on her head. Involuntarily, I start to gag, repulsed by the sight of her decayed skin and corn-husk hair.

Lilith sinks to the ground and starts to weep. Dr. Sato rushes to get her tissues. She clutches the box, hyperventilating.

I want to run to Helen, to breathe life into her. Or awaken her with brute force. I imagine pummeling her chest with the music in my fingertips until it starts a rhythm of its own.

"I am so sorry for your loss," Dr. Sato says. "I have to ask you to confirm her identity."

My voice falters. "I think it's her," I say.

He shows us her driver's license. A sob rises in my throat.

"You can see why I needed to be sure." He takes a step closer to us. "I don't mean to be insensitive, but was she on anything?"

Lilith shakes her head, tears splattering around her. "No," she says firmly. "No way."

I hesitate, wondering if I should correct her. Helen, Lilith, and I are all technically on a lot of things.

"Was she sick?" I ask. "She must have been sick." My voice cracks. I gesture at the picture. "She looked like this last week."

Dr. Sato eyes me with faint mistrust. "With your permission, we'd like to run tests. Our guess is that she must have been taking something. Repeatedly."

I look down at my feet. "Is that how she died? If I can ask?"

"Her body had grown accustomed to a substance we need to identify. Oddly, the substance that was killing her might also have been what was keeping her alive until the end. A kind of learned dependence by the body. Do you know if Helen frequented any construction sites? Was she doing renovations of any kind?"

"I can't think of anything," I say.

"She was surrounded by detritus when she arrived. We took the liberty of doing some preliminary testing on the miscellany, not thinking they would be chunks of her lungs. We've seen lung-function impairment before, of course, though certainly not to this degree, and only in the bodies of people who have worked in heavy construction for decades." He sighs at the blank looks on our faces. "The markings we found were consistent with the respiratory scarring we see from particulates, asbestosis, crystalline silica. Her lungs were inflamed by bits of bone and plaster that were slowly expanding. They would have killed her eventually if she didn't die of natural causes first. Extranatural, that is. There's too much organic material in her. Globs of stuff, clogging everything, interacting and counteracting in unpredictable ways."

I am dumbfounded by this information.

"Let me ask you something. My colleagues and I have been exhaustively running through any and all possible explanations for her symptoms. To be quite frank, we're stumped. The only thing that could begin to explain the level of damage . . . is, well. This might be a strange question, but she worked at Holistik, right? Is it possible Holistik is testing on human subjects?"

CHAPTER TWENTY-THREE

ilith and I leave together. I take big gulps of the fresh air in the hallway. She motions for me to follow her into a bathroom. By the sink, she starts shaking violently before throwing up on the floor.

"It's OK," I say, pulling her up by the arm. I feel sick, looking at her green spongy puke.

She rinses her mouth with the faucet before speaking.

"I need to ask you about something."

"What is it?"

"I found something. With your name on it." Lilith pulls a packet of papers from her bag. She does her best to uncrumple them before splaying them by the sink.

The first page is torn. A list of women's names.

"Do you recognize any of these names?"

I take a closer look but shake my head. "Do you?"

Lilith nods. "Not all of them, but a few. They're on payroll. I've never met them before, but the names I know belong to people who work at the Gunks."

The next few pages are a contract of some kind. I skim the contents, my attention catching on certain clauses.

(a) Volunteer agrees that all processes and products Volunteer is exposed to are confidential and may not be divulged in any manner whatsoever by Volunteer to any third parties (including, without limitation, newspapers, periodicals, magazines, other publications, television and radio stations, websites, blogs, social media, and/or any employees, contractors, or associates thereof, or any other individual or corporation), except as may be authorized in advance by the Company in writing or as otherwise required by law, with notice to the Company.

. . .

(4) Volunteer agrees that any remedy that Volunteer has in public courts is waived indefinitely and that any actions brought against Volunteer or by Volunteer will be settled by private arbitration with the arbitrators elected out of the Board of Biological and Experimental Ethics in Geneva, Switzerland, by the Company, all costs of which are to be defrayed against Volunteer's wages and assets.

. . .

(g) Volunteer understands their inventions, copyrights, biological information, experimental data, and biological product are the intellectual property of the Company, during the extent of the relationship between Volunteer and the Company, including, but without limitation, any experimental follow-up period that may arise.

. . .

(iii) Volunteer understands and assumes the risk of and exempts the Company from any possible side effects whether or not expressly defined, including but not limited to prolonged headaches, drowsiness, internal discomfort and

cramping, rapid weight loss, short-term memory loss, syndac-
tyly, vivid dreams, elongated incisors, decrystallization of
bone tissue, spontaneous zygote multiplication, heightened
post-gestational depression, homicidal tendencies, heightened
sensitivity to light.

Following this contract is what appears to be an old advertise-
ment. On the discolored page, a pregnant woman is sleeping with
a big smile on her face while a nurse waits between her legs with
outstretched arms.

The last page is another list of names, this time titled
Apothecare.

Lilith's eyes pierce mine. "This is what I wanted to show you."

She runs a finger down the piece of paper, stopping at my
name.

Next to my name are the words *good candidate for Skintellect
and Everlasting.* I've seen this piece of paper before, but I can't
place where.

"Where did you find this?" I ask her.

"I used to smoke. With Henry, when we were together."

I cough, trying to swallow my surprise.

"After you left last night, I was so nervous. I needed something to calm myself, so I looked for cigarettes in his old hiding
spots and found this instead. What's Apothecare?"

"It's the other job I have. It's part of Organic Provisions. Saje
runs it."

"What do you do?"

"Well, I guess, sex work."

"Sex work?"

"Yeah. Organic, all-natural sex work."

Lilith looks at me dubiously.

I hear it, too, now that I'm saying it out loud for the first time. Since when does sex need any help being organic or all-natural?

"That's a new one." She sighs, looking back at the papers.

"Is this paperwork from Organic Provisions?"

Lilith has a grim expression. "I don't know. It just says 'the Company' on the papers."

"Should we tell someone about this?" I ask.

"Who would believe us? And what would we even say?"

She's right, I think to myself. Someone in the hall walks past the bathroom, and their footsteps echo the persistent thunk of a deer hoof, knocking loose the memory of where I had already seen that list of names.

"They might be watching us," Lilith says before I can tell her about the house in the Gunks.

"Who?"

"Organic Provisions." She is speaking so softly I can barely hear her over the running water. "I have to go. We shouldn't leave together. Wait at least five minutes after I'm gone, OK?" She fluffs her bangs, smiling emptily in the mirror before turning toward the exit.

I go into a stall and lock the door. Sit on the toilet and allow myself to cry. I don't know how much time passes. When I finally stand and unlock the door, my face looks like the crumpled red balloon no one wants to buy at a drugstore.

When I leave the bathroom, I hear a strange sound coming from where Helen is being kept. I look through the window, upset that someone is laughing so uninhibitedly. But it is Henry in the room, crying hysterically while grabbing the shoulders of Helen's unresponsive body.

"Wake up wake up wake up!" he screams. "Oh god, oh god, oh god. It's all my fault. What do I do now? Tell me what to do! Please! I'm so sorry, Helen, I'm so sorry I'm so sorry I'm so sorry I'm so sorry."

Dr. Sato walks in with security guards. Instinctively, I lower myself so as not to be seen by them.

"What are you doing here?" Dr. Sato asks Henry.

"I'm . . . her twin," Henry chokes out between guttural cries.

Dr. Sato motions for the security guards to take hold of Henry. "He's lying. Her twin was just here," Dr. Sato says to them.

I turn abruptly and leave Bellevue.

I don't have much time before Wilden is supposed to take me to my next Apothecare appointment. I start walking, trying to find some distance from Bellevue. I listen to the people around me deep in conversation about everyday things and can't understand how Helen's death hasn't fundamentally altered everyone else. How can people make dinner plans when the world has pitched into darkness? I would give anything to go back to a time before I had lost Helen. I would give anything to go home. Not the place I share with Alice and Charlie, but the home I lived in with my parents. The one I had to give up after their accident. Crumbling plaster beneath yellowing wallpaper, the mulberry tree at the end of the block that Ma picked for tea.

In my memory, she is always making an extra cup for me. In a couple of minutes, she will bring me the tea on a little tray with apple slices and set it down on the piano bench next to me. I'll take a break to eat, and she'll remove her slippers to sit on the couch and sip tea with me. A confused sound comes from her mouth as it twists to one side. She drops the cup in her right hand and pins both arms to her body, shriveling until she looks like the immobile woman I visit at Applebaum.

I swipe at the tears that have formed in the corners of my eyes and choose a restaurant nearby for pickup. I order a tea while waiting for Wilden and notice the barista eyeing me warily. I must look and smell terrible. In their tiny urine-caked bathroom, I slather on a thick honey moisturizer from Holistik. My hands tremble while rubbing the product into my skin. Images of Helen bubble over in my mind. I try to focus on the details around me as a way of distracting myself. I note the bits of food stuck to the stained sink, some of it lodged in the drain. Brown flecks cover the mirror. Dried blood? A few pimples on my chin. I know what Madison and the other girls would say if they saw me. Blemishes are a symptom of poison in the mind. A sweep of Holistik concealer and the imperfections vanish instantly. If only there was a product capable of quieting the irrepressible fear that what happened to Helen could happen to me, is maybe already happening to me.

CHAPTER TWENTY-FOUR

"What makes it so shiny?" I ask.

The woman is rubbing the viscous cream into my thighs, inadvertently giving my tired limbs a welcome massage. "Could be various things, but most likely the natural adhesive that comes from mussels and oysters."

Since my initial engagement at Apothecare, there has been no more costuming. No more exaggerated hair or makeup. They simply coat me in the dewy sweet-smelling salve, and the next thing I remember is waking up at home.

I am very cold. I try a few times to open my eyes. I seem to be lying on a hard bed in a room surrounded by glass. My sweat has soaked the sheet beneath me. Beyond the glass, shadows move occasionally. There are people reclining on my right, draped like melted wax on red couches. Their faces are blurry. I hear a faint tapping sound. Something is dripping on me. I look up to see an ornate silver sculpture looming over my body. Metallic arms and a funnel of some kind.

"Start to lower," says a voice to my right.

The object starts moving toward me. As it gets closer, I realize my hands and legs are restrained. In fact, I can't move at all. Or maybe my body is moving, but I am outside of it.

"Easy, easy. OK, hold on. Let's scan it back."

The silver thing whizzes from my stomach area to stop by my feet. I see it more clearly now. A thin metal sheath containing something mottled brown, floppy, and long. An extremity of some kind, capped in silver along the sides and wriggling.

I hear the same voice, speaking urgently now, "Approach, approach, stop! OK, now enter. Keep going, keep going."

I feel a shock of cold as something gelatinous slithers inside my vagina. It presses against the walls. I feel faint.

"Release," the voice says.

A loud hissing sound starts, drowning out what the voice is saying before I feel an excruciating pain. Something is inside me, alternately clenching and flooding me with liquid. I want to scream. I try to scream. A man's face swims into view. I hear him over the steam.

"Hey, her eyes are open. Is that normal?"

I try to shut my eyes.

Hurried footsteps, and the man says, "I swear they were a second ago."

Another voice, from farther away, "With all that scopy? No way."

I feel myself being moved. They are wheeling me somewhere.

A woman starts speaking. "How is she doing?"

"Good," another voice says. "But we need to keep a close eye. This is only her second injection, so it probably won't take. Even with the new modifications, the sperm is not being welcomed. We may have to try using a Crocuta pseudo-penis as a tool for the insemination. Octopus mothers die giving birth, and that seems to be influencing the women once they've been implanted. It's a similar response to postpartum depression, but quite unmanageable because of how many eggs are released and fertilized. I would guess both women who killed themselves last month were severely depressed after losing their broods. We just didn't catch it in time. We're researching ways to cut off the natural biological responses, but the current rotation needs to be under constant watch until we know more. In the meantime, we have a couple more hectocotyli ready to go for the others."

By the time he finishes talking, his voice is very quiet, as if someone is slowly dimming the volume on him.

The heat in the store is oppressive. Madison has locked me in from the outside. Giant leaves press against the windows of sweating glass, drilling their roots through cracks in the wall and spilling through. Lush tropical flowers bloom around me in the shape of desperate hands, scratching to get in. Emerson and Tanner ruffle their feathers and hawk acid phlegm, screeching at me for the bright orange acrylics growing from my fingertips in long curlicues as milky globules drop from between my legs. Businessmen in their suits squat near me with glazed eyes and knife-sharp beaks, pecking at the tapioca dribbling from me.

"Help!" I shout, unable to move from the weight of the acrylics, now extending to the other side of the store. No one can hear me over the scratchy hiss the nails make on the floor as they grow.

"Are these men bothering you?" Victor has come up the stairs, looking at me with a kind, efficient expression. He rubs his eye and starts to extract something from it. A thin white feather, followed by another and another and another. He is almost all bird when he pins me to the ground with his talons and covers me with a shining white cream.

CHAPTER TWENTY-FIVE

hear someone knocking from far away and travel from the depths of unconsciousness to the surface. I am not in my own bed. It must be one of the overnight rooms at Apothecare. I start to cry with relief. I can still feel the horrible violation, the slithering from my dream. There is a crust of blood on my legs, and the sheets beneath me look like they have been doused in wine. Is it possible the dream was real? I feel between my thighs for the slick strands there, wet with mucus and grainy with broken skin. Shaking, I focus on taking deep breaths.

I have to talk to Lilith as soon as possible. My phone is on the pillow beside me. I am reaching for it when I hear Saje's voice. My head pulses when I stand. There is a folded robe at the edge of the bed. I cover myself, open the door, and walk toward what I recognize to be an entrance to the golden room. Saje's voice suddenly appears, much closer. On instinct, I duck through the nearest doorway, where I find a girl drowsing.

She is partially dressed in a Japanese schoolgirl costume. Underneath the wide collar and red bow, her breasts flop on the bed. She doesn't stir when I enter, so I stay in her room and peer through the small opening in the door.

"Is the procedure invasive?" a voice is saying from the hallway.

"It's not invasive at all. The women feel absolutely nothing during insemination or extraction. We don't use any traditionally harmful anesthetics, if that's a concern. We made a proprietary embrocation inspired by an amnesiac state used for childbirth in the 1800s. The brood takes or it doesn't. Either way, they go on with their lives," Saje says.

The other woman jokes, "You mean you don't kill them?"

They both laugh.

"I just—I don't want to push, but it's been a year since our very generous donation, and Tommy and I aren't getting any younger. He's been talking about having a conventional surrogacy. I know the numbers are confidential, but is there anything you can share about the success rate or when it might be available?"

"Cresslyn, I assure you Everlasting is worth the wait. The numbers are still under wraps, but not for much longer. I can guarantee that you'll have more information within a month or two. In the meantime, Skintellect will be ready for booking next week. That formula has already undergone significant testing. The skin color on all test subjects adapted exactly as predicted."

"Saje, all I want is a baby. I feel like I'm finally ready to be a mother. I wish my body would cooperate, but that's where you come in. As great as Skintellect sounds, I'm not interested. I'm sure you've noticed that I've suspended all of my procedural subscriptions at Holistik? Let's get back to Everlasting. How are the women selected? Or are they volunteers?"

A heavy sigh from Saje. "It's a rigorous process. We usually start with girls who specialize in different artistic endeavors. It helps us make good on our promise of intelligent and creative children. Of course the chosen women are beautiful. Victor certainly makes sure of that." Saje laughs. "And they are compensated handsomely."

I move my head back and forth to see if I can pinpoint where they are. A large yellow-rimmed eye floats into my field of vision.

"Oh," Saje says softly. "Here's one of them now."

She opens the door, and I step through it automatically. The girl in the bed is apparently undisturbed as Saje firmly closes the door behind me.

A beautiful woman around my age with thin blond hair stands next to Saje, staring at me covetously with amber eyes. "Hi, what's your name?"

Saje laughs like her question is a funny one. "We can't release that kind of information; we have to protect our girls! But as you can see, she's here, real and perfectly lovely."

I smile awkwardly as she reaches out a hand and rubs a strand of my hair between her fingers.

"She's an incredible pianist, I have to tell you. Studied at the Conservatory."

The woman looks at me with undisguised surprise. "Really!"

Saje smiles graciously. "It's like I said before. We only have the best working for us. Anyway, we should probably end our meeting here. And Cresslyn, the other girls will be jealous if they hear about this little tour, so let's keep this between us, hmm? You can call me if you have any other concerns. You know your way out, of course."

The blond woman walks away, her chic heels clinking down the hall. The door to the golden room opens, and I am left alone with Saje.

"I hope you don't mind. We kept you overnight because you

were sleeping so deeply, and we didn't want to disturb you." She strokes a few of the damp hairs on my head, assessing me from head to toe. "You need a bath and a change of clothes. The ghee vats have just been freshly filled if you want to use one of the bathtubs upstairs? No? I'll call for Wilden to bring you home. Have you, by any chance, been in touch with Lilith?"

She says this casually while smoothing the hair on my forehead. I smile at her as dreamily as I can and shake my head. Her nails, which are filed to a point in the center of each finger, are sharp against my temple.

CHAPTER TWENTY-SIX

have never been to Lilith's place before. I feign an appetite and ask Wilden to drop me off at a café by her place on the Lower East Side. Truthfully, I have often wondered where Lilith lives. She dresses with such apparent wealth; I have always assumed her living situation to be similarly flush. Instead, she welcomes me into a tiny studio apartment that smells faintly of tomato sauce. There is an unmade bed in one corner, and the rest of the apartment is dedicated to a small kitchen and a desk crammed with newspaper articles and printouts, all having to do with Organic Provisions, Holistik, and Victor. There are even documents taped to the wall, next to beautiful sketches I recognize to be the work of Helen.

I find myself at her desk, looking through the things collected there, some of which seem very old. A picture of Victor grins at me from a profile written in the early '90s.

"What is all this?" I ask.

"I know it looks crazy," she says.

"That's not what I said."

"I was a journalist. Before Holistik." She shrugs. "It feels like a lifetime ago now. But initially, I started working at Holistik because I thought there was a big story there."

"Clearly, you were onto something," I say. The dream from last night slinks across my mind. "Why haven't you published anything? It seems like you have enough information, especially with the papers you found?"

Lilith snorts. "You don't think I've tried? Media outlets won't approach me with a ten-foot pole unless I have people who are willing to go on record." She looks down, suddenly self-conscious. "I lost my first job and a couple of internships because I kept pushing for a story on Holistik. My old boss said they couldn't trust my journalistic integrity, called it a personal vendetta. And then, of course, I found out Victor owns the site. How stupid am I? He owns so many of them. He can and has shut up an infinite number of people. Even people who aren't working for him anymore. How many times have I set up an interview with an ex-employee, only to have them ghost me? I need unassailable proof, people willing to go on record who won't be persuaded by money. I mean, what do I even really know at this point? I know people who work out at the Gunks mysteriously disappear. I know Organic Provisions is bigger than just Holistik, that it includes your weird sex club. At the end of the day, everything I know can be dismissed too easily as hearsay."

Lilith looks exhausted.

I open my mouth, wanting to offer myself as a name or source to her. It snaps shut when I remember my parents. There is no denying that I have also been muzzled by a dependence on money.

I drop the profile of Victor back onto the desk and touch a drawing of Lilith that Helen must have sketched.

She joins me in front of the drawing but looks at me instead. "God. You look just like her, don't you?" Lilith says, starting to cry.

She buries her face in my chest, and I wrap my arms around her. Try to hold her together. She looks up at me, her dark green eyes kaleidoscopic from the tears streaking down her cheeks.

She starts kissing me. My body responds first, less confused than my mind. I kiss back, registering the texture of her soft lips on mine. Tentatively, I run the back of my hand up and down the length of her arm as she reaches a palm under my shirt. Her hand moves slowly upward, circling a breast with her fingertips.

It feels nice to leave my body, to register feelings that are external. The night at the Cloisters awakened something in me, I had assumed for Helen, but maybe also for Lilith. Her fast fingers slipping inside me, her eyes coldly assessing me. I don't want to admit it, but there has always been something arousing about her disdain for me, a shame I want to bury my face in. But with my eyes closed, all I can see is Helen's heart-shaped face. I start to feel guilty, as if Helen is in the room watching us. *You shouldn't be doing this. You should be with me.* Or, more likely, *She should be with me.* I push Lilith away and cry out in surprise. I hadn't imagined it. Above the cramped kitchen nook, there is a detailed sketch of Helen. I sink to the ground, upset by how well it captures her. Lilith kneels, sitting next to me, and we look at Helen together.

We fall asleep on her bed awhile later, spooning so neither of us can see how badly the other is crying.

I wake to her pressing into me. It is easier to finish what we started in the dark, where we can forget who we are with. She touches me roughly, almost with anger, and I am quick to come thinking of the times she and Helen have done this. What I lack in experience I make up for in patience, licking her gently until she shudders, falling back. We lie in her bed afterward in silence.

She flicks my stomach with her finger. "I love her."

I try not to be hurt or even surprised by this admission.

"I'm just saying, don't get any ideas. This is a distraction for me. You might look like her, but you aren't her."

She falls asleep soon after, curled in a little ball away from me. I watch the sun rise, illuminating Helen's sketch through the window before I succumb to exhaustion.

For the first few minutes of wakefulness, I don't remember Helen is gone. Then I see her in front of me. The sun is blazing now, and long fingers of light reach through the window as if to extinguish her. The loss hits me, sharp and sudden. I can't stand to be around Helen's drawing any longer, so I grab my things and leave the apartment.

I walk for hours without any awareness of the time or distance. The moon is still visible, a fingernail clipping tossed into the sky. I imagine climbing onto its thin ledge and jumping. The opening of Prokofiev's Piano Sonata no. 6 plays in my head. I had worked on it in my last few years at the Conservatory, along with his other War Sonatas. No one had assigned them to me, but I was fascinated by their difficulty. Not only their technical difficulty and the stamina it would take to master them, but also the emotional difficulty of facing them. Of surviving them. I suppose the music has appeared in my mind now to comfort me, to remind me that no one is alone in grief.

At home, I scrub Lilith from my body in Alice and Charlie's shower. The white space of the bathtub is comforting, and I try to fill my mind with its blankness. I step out of the shower and stare at myself in the mirror. My skin is peppered with minuscule bumps. My nose widens at the nostrils. With so much happening the last few days, I haven't been as scrupulous with my skin care. I go downstairs and try to remedy the damage. The bumps immediately retract with the application of a light face serum. I grab my supplement jars from under the sink, seeing with fresh eyes the sheer number of pills I take every day. I wonder briefly if I can try taking a few key products instead of all of them. I turn the faucet on and swallow that thought along with my pills. My face had just demonstrated how quickly things can change.

"Lilith?"

She had called multiple times while I was in the shower.

"Are you going to work today?" she asks.

I don't say anything.

"Listen. I think . . . were you . . . followed yesterday?"

"What do you mean?"

"To my place. I think someone has been here. After you left, while I was out."

"I didn't notice. I'm sorry if—"

"No, it's not your fault. I just wanted to ask in case you noticed anything." She sighs. "Are you going into work today or not?"

I had been avoiding thinking about it. "I guess so. I don't want to, but I will. Something weird might have happened the other night at Apothecare. I can't stop thinking about it."

"What do you mean, 'weird'? Why didn't you mention it yesterday?"

"I'm not sure. I didn't . . . still don't really know how to explain it. Can we talk when I get in?"

"I won't be at Holistik today. I'm meeting with Saje in the Gunks. She and Victor want my help planning the service. They also want me to take over some of Helen's responsibilities out there. I figure it'll be a good way for me to get an eye on the area, look for some of the names we saw on that list. Let's meet tonight when I get back."

When Lilith and I hang up, I check my email. Another reminder from Applebaum that I haven't paid the astronomical price for the transfer of my parents to the hospital and back.

I have a message, too, from an unknown number asking to meet: *Sorry I didn't get in touch sooner. Any chance you're free for lunch?*

Who is this? I respond.

Conor Hearst.

CHAPTER TWENTY-SEVEN

When I arrive at the store, there is a line of customers wrapped around the block. Spring is just beginning in earnest, and there is a feeling of anticipation in the air. Inside, most of the retail staff are sitting around. Madison is downstairs drinking one of her supplements in the employee area. She waves me over.

"What's going on today? Why is everyone here?" I ask her.

"The ducklings are hatching now."

All day, an endless line outside of Holistik. I watch as Emerson hands a tall, tanned couple a pair of blindfolded ducklings at the back of the store. They hold the downy bodies close to their chests and listen to the training specialist before they untie the blindfolds and make eye contact with their new adorable balls of fluff. These ducklings are the latest in emotional support technology, bred for the specific purpose of imprinting on humans for therapeutic benefits.

I feel as if I've only just arrived at work when it's time for my break.

Downstairs, Tanner is unpacking new shipments with a grimace on her face. "It's not fair. The Santa Monica clients got fawns and Seoul got foxes. These won't shut up!"

The chirping of the newborn ducklings, blindfolded and separated from their mothers, is driving her crazy. She watches enviously as I walk up the stairs. Conor and I have agreed to meet at a small café nearby. He is already seated, staring ahead, expressionless. Warmth floods his face when he sees me. He gets up and unexpectedly gives me a hug.

"I still can't get over how different you look," he says, shaking his head. He picks up a lock of hair from my shoulder. "The blond looks good on you."

I smile uneasily. It had been gradual enough that I almost hadn't noticed, but it was true. The hair on my head had lightened considerably. We exchange pleasantries about the weather, and he orders lunch. He eyes the food I bring out of my tote. I explain Holistik's stringent policies on facial care, hygiene, and nutrition to him.

"Is that legal? I mean, why wouldn't you want these amazing things, but they can't actually require you to take stuff, can they?"

I feel stupid for never having thought about it. "I don't know," I say truthfully. "I'm not sure anyone has ever cared to ask."

He shrugs. "It's certainly a famous place to work if you're going to slum it in retail."

A waitress brings his sandwich, and he picks at it.

"Are you playing at all?"

I shake my head.

"Did you stop because of your parents?"

Now it's my turn to pick at the salad in front of me. The leaves are still springy and fresh despite being in my tote, unrefrigerated for days. Produce from the Gunks is remarkable.

"Yes."

He nods thoughtfully and ducks his head. "I'll never forget having to be the one to tell you."

I smile at him a little. "I'm glad it was you."

He clears his throat. "There wasn't another reason?" His light blue eyes plead with mine for an answer.

"Why?"

He grips the table with his hands as if to steady himself. "This is a bit embarrassing, but I've started seeing a therapist."

"That's not embarrassing at all. It's great," I say.

"I'm remembering things. Including—" He pauses. "I'm sorry for the way we treated you at the Conservatory."

That's what this is about. I sigh with relief. "It was a long time ago and we were all so young. Don't worry about it."

"No. It's not OK. What we did was awful," he whispers. He takes something from the backpack beside him and places it on the table between us. "We should never have taken it."

I close a hand over the photo that was stolen from my room years ago. My heart pounds. "Thank you," I say.

He looks at me miserably. "It was Genevieve's idea. My girl-friend at the time. But I shouldn't have gone along with it. I'm so glad I bumped into you that day. I've kept it just in case."

I lean back and breathe, pressing the photo against my chest.

"It's not just that. Other things have come up," he continues.

I nod, trying to encourage him. All I want now is time alone with the photo.

"Bad things. And I don't know if they're real or not."

"Like what?"

Drops of sweat are blooming on his forehead. He's shaking, too, and I feel like I'm seeing something I'm not supposed to see. Conor was always such a poised and controlled performer.

"I think . . ." He pauses and scratches his hands. "I think they did something to you. Maybe the other girls, too, and to me. I'm not sure. Do you remember anything out of the ordinary?"

I try to think back to the early days at the Conservatory. As usual, I'm not able to remember much. Too many notes, pieces, and people in the audience crowd my mind.

"Do you remember the cream we used for our hands? In Zsa's studio?"

I nod slowly.

"I know this sounds crazy, but I wonder if there was something in it. There's too much . . . time missing." Conor's hands are agitated, running through his hair. "There's an image I keep seeing. From one of the donor events we used to play together."

I get the feeling, suddenly, that something terrible will happen if he doesn't stop speaking.

"You remember, don't you? When Zsaborsky would take us out on weekends?" he says.

I remember the weekends but can't recall his presence at any of them. I answer as honestly as I can without hurting his feelings. "I feel like I can't remember as much as I should. I'm close to it, but—"

"It's through a door, or a membrane, and you can't pass through."

"Yes."

At my response, he pushes his sandwich away from him, knotting his hands together. "The image. You're on top of a piano, somewhere I don't recognize. You look like you're sleeping, and above you, there's a man with very long hair."

When I return to Holistik, I am shaky and distracted. Conor and I had switched to lighter topics by the end of our stilted conversation, but what he shared weighs on me. I have a few hours between my shift at Holistik and my next Apothecare session. I decide to clear my mind by going for walk.

I put on my headphones and listen to the Beethoven quartet so beloved by my dad.

I went to a performance of Beethoven's *Grosse Fugue* once, the movement that comes directly after the one Ba played for me. The musicians had seemed so in touch with each other, I thought they must have been clairvoyant. I was mesmerized by their fingertips contorting on the tightropes of their silver strings.

I remembered thinking I had found magic. I imagined relationships, societies, communities in touch with one another's feelings. It would be a kind of Utopia. As a solo pianist, I had often been sad that I could never be part of a string quartet. They learn how to breathe together, live together, and, most impressively, communicate with each other without words.

That night after the concert, I sat at the piano as I usually did and stared at my fingers. Holding my soft flesh to the unyielding keys, I had never felt so alone.

I take the train home to get ready for my Apothecare session. It's still early in the afternoon, so there are plenty of empty seats in the subway car. I sit down and take the photo from my bag. It is more faded now, but there we all are. Ma and Ba are smiling and holding me tightly. A piece of music unspools in my mind as I process the feeling of seeing my parents then with the knowledge of who they are now. *Beklemmt.* In the picture, we are backstage at a small regional competition in upstate New York. I am wearing an old-fashioned velvet dress with a large floral pattern and ruched sleeves down to my wrists. I stand next to a piano with one hand awkwardly on the keys and my parents by my side. We are happy because I have just won. Soon the car will come, offering me a spot at the Conservatory. Behind us, a tall man with a curtain of long hair stands, smiling at something out of frame. My stomach lurches, though the train is moving steadily. He is much younger in the photo, but this must have been how he looked before any of his procedures.

CHAPTER TWENTY-EIGHT

When I get home, I open my computer and find a flood of emails from Applebaum. Later. I'll figure it out later. I toast a couple of spirulina Pop-Tarts and try calling Lilith a few times when an unknown number appears on my screen.

"Hello?"

"Hi, is this the daughter of Mei-Lan and Li Zhou?"

"This is she."

"You may not remember me. A few months ago, I ran some tests at the Applebaum Care Facility for your parents."

My heart sinks.

"Do you have a moment to talk? I have some questions for you."

"Sure," I say uneasily.

"What is your ethnicity?"

"I'm Chinese. Chinese American."

"That's what I thought." He hesitates on the other end. "And are there any specific dietary supplements? Special celebration foods that are a part of your culture?"

"Do you mean like mooncake? Things like that?"

The doctor sighs. He seems to gather himself before carrying on. "We can now say with certainty that your parents had advanced kuru. All the symptoms were there. Sudden dementia, poor coordination, and, of course, the twitching and trembling for which kuru is named. It's such a rare disease, it took us too—"

"How would they have gotten it?" I have never heard of this disease before.

"That's why I asked about dietary customs. You see, kuru is typically associated with . . . with . . . cannibalism. It takes years to incubate, but since your parents were already immunocompromised—"

"Excuse me?" *Cannibalism?* "Of course they aren't cannibals," I finally say in disbelief. "That has *never* been part of our culture."

"I apologize for how that must have sounded," the doctor says quickly. "I didn't ask because of your ethnicity, but because we took the liberty of testing the supplements they had been ingesting regularly. Most of them are from a place called Holistik—are you familiar with that brand?"

It takes me a moment to find my voice. "I work there."

"I see."

A long silence on the other end.

"The ingredients listed on these Holistik jars are all commonly used by the beauty industry with the exception of a few experimental herbs. Because of your parents' highly specific and, frankly, alarming symptoms, we ran tests on them as a precaution. It's a good thing we did. The labels are inaccurate. One of my colleagues has several of the same Holistik products, so we ran comparative samples. This is where things get really bizarre.

"The products she bought from the store and the products

being taken by your parents were completely different, despite their identical labels." Another sigh. "Ms. Zhou? Everything your parents were taking had traces of human bone and flesh."

I gag, remembering a cold hand on my plump cheek. A long red hair in congealing yolk.

Whatever the birds pick clean, we find a use for. Zero-waste and all. You saw the pits, didn't you?

Suddenly, I register what he said. "I'm sorry, what do you mean, 'were'? Why are you saying 'were'?"

I ask the question, but I already know.

"I'm sorry." He sounds flustered. "Someone from the facility was supposed to contact you. I didn't realize."

I remove the phone from my ear and look at it in my hand. He starts speaking again, but I hang up.

Hours pass. Eventually, I become aware of the wetness of my face and the hoarseness of my throat, but I don't remember the sobbing or the screaming. My chest is shaking so much I don't realize at first that my mandala is convulsing. Wilden will be here soon. I want to call it off, quit Apothecare and Holistik. Without my parents, there is no point.

The mandala is starting to singe my skin. I flip it open, but the pills fall and roll under the fridge. Somehow, it must know I haven't taken them because it continues to burn. I try to yank it over my head, but it won't fit. A knife lies rusting on the counter. I reach for it and lunge at the little sphere, nicking the soft skin above my collarbone. The dainty chain and pendant are impervious.

I run to my bathroom downstairs and fumble in the dingy

space under the sink. I fill my shaking hand with pills and open the tap. The cool water clears my head, dispersing a thunderous headache. I think of the white-flecked apron Helen wore while doing ceramics. I think of the ice cream she made for me, that first dinner we had, and the yellow sliver I put in my pocket. The twisted shapes of her Gunks supply. The same substances I took once, twice, and then repeatedly to my parents for their recovery.

Helen's last words to me: *Stop taking everything.* It was a command.

I tilt my left hand and spill the pellets into the drain. I instantly feel more lucid. A pack of unopened razors in the shower catches my eye. Where the knife was too dull, a fresh razor succeeds. The silver droplet falls with a wet thud, transforming into a shapeless gray gel again. It left a small crater of burned flesh at the base of my throat. I shut the tap and gaze at myself in the mirror. Buttery skin, light gold hair, and a straight, slightly upturned nose.

You might look like her, but you aren't her, Lilith had said.

A comment that had stung and confused me in the moment because I hadn't wanted to acknowledge how much I had been changing. In the last year, I had slowly transformed into someone else. Now the resemblance is uncanny. Helen has come back to life through me.

I touch a soft downy cheek. Tuck a gilded ringlet behind my ear as I admire my new self. This is, after all, the face I loved. I can admit that to myself now. I feel honored. Chosen. Looking down at my hands, I admire these new implements, too. They are so much longer than my own. The opening of Rachmaninoff's Piano Concerto no. 3 sounds in my head, how much easier his works will be with the additional length. I place my hands on the edge of the sink and pretend to play. The ivory fingers mash together, twisting and tangling in ways I can't correct or command. They are beautiful, but they might as well be made of the marble they resemble. I am repulsed, suddenly, by my thoughts. Helen can't live on in me any more than I can as her. I look in the mirror again. This time, I don't see Helen's presence as much as I see the absence of my parents.

Gone are my mother's small black eyes, as dark as the watermelon seeds we loved to eat together. My father's slightly squashed nose. That slow shy smile of his I sometimes catch on my face. Gone are my mother's neat compact hands, too short and stubby to be ideal for piano, but limber and strong, with skill cultivated over years of labor. Gone are the gentle slopes of my mother's sturdy body. Ba's stocky calves. In their place are lean muscled runners' legs. My father's flat feet have curved into Helen's high arches. Without them, how can I be sure of following in his footsteps?

The only thing that had given me any measure of comfort when they had their accident was the idea of inheritance. Their DNA unfolding quietly in my body. A gesture here, a habitual tic there. A part of me was always waiting for them. For my temples to silver like my mother's, stars shooting through midnight hair. For my body to gather in the swells of soft skin I clutched as a child. I hoped I would laugh one day, and it would be an echo of my father's joy.

Now they are truly gone. And it is my fault. The thought has been needling its way through my brain. The supplements. The unanswered questions because they were unasked. A kind of lethargy had settled on me at the Conservatory, turned into impotence by every additional place that relegated me an outsider. I had decided that everyone else knew best. Now I have lost not only my culture but my family as well.

I am tearing at the gold curls that tumble relentlessly from my head when I notice it. The big tub wedged between the sink and the bathtub. I pick it up. Even unopened, I can smell the potent herbs Ma always got at the Chinese grocery store to add to the Vaseline. Helen looks at me from the mirror. She whispers: *You know what you have to do, right?*

CHAPTER TWENTY-NINE

try to stay awake in the car, but my eyelids flutter. I focus on the air vents, and then on Wilden, indecipherable as usual behind the thick glass that separates us.

"Ms. Anna, we're here."

I get out of the car shakily, groggy as usual from the nap I didn't want to take, and make my way to the golden room.

Astrid comes to greet me, fingering the limp strands of my hair with a look of revulsion. "Are you OK? You seem . . . anxious?"

That's not good. I shake my head apologetically. "I didn't sleep well last night. Could I have some tea?"

When we reach the bathing area, Astrid goes to get the tea. No one is around. I dip my hair in the water, making sure nothing else gets wet.

Astrid returns as I'm tightening the sash of my robe. "That was fast!" she says brightly.

I smile back, trying to match her wattage.

The man and woman are there, ready with the cream. I take off the robe and they start to rub. I tell myself I'm being paranoid.

"What am I wearing today?" I ask, hoping to take attention away from my structured breathing.

"Same as usual. You get to be yourself," the woman says wryly. As she speaks, she slaps the light rose-gold balm on me more roughly than usual. "It isn't staying. Did you bathe in the lake?"

I force my head up and down. I can feel my lower chin starting to tremble. The thin layer of Vaseline I applied to my skin is giving her trouble, but I want to stay awake this time and hope the Vaseline will act as a barrier against anything meant to slip quietly into my bloodstream. I need to know with certainty what they are doing, and then Lilith and I can go to the authorities.

Finally, they're somewhat satisfied. I enter the decontamination chamber and a light air blows on me. There are double doors at the far end of the room. I stop breathing when I realize the substance I'm inhaling is causing me to feel faint. The wind dies down and Astrid comes in from the other side to collect me. I am certain she can hear my heart pounding. I make my body as soft and pliant as possible so she can steer me easily. I try not to walk too fast or seem too purposeful with my steps. We enter a small room, almost a hospital waiting area, where two men are gathered.

"It's been about five minutes since the twilight was applied and about fifteen since she was in the water, so it should be kicking in full-force right about now." Astrid taps the door twice. "Good luck," she says, on her way out.

I stand where she left me, not sure if I should keep my eyes open. I make my face rigid with a vague docility and stare straight ahead at the men who are staring back.

They take me to another room. This one is much bigger, with a hospital bed in the middle and complicated machinery around it. I recognize the silver structure dangling like a steampunk chandelier above the bed. So it wasn't a dream. They lead me to the bed and help me onto it, one man aggressively squeezing my thighs as he lifts me. It seems my acting is working.

I lie on the table, and one of them says to me, "Your eyes are heavy, and you feel sleepy. You decide to take a nap now."

I close my eyes, careful not to furrow my eyebrows. I listen as they position things around me, maneuvering utensils on a pan before they place my arms and feet in clamps. An object hangs over me, holding something slick with metal-tipped suction cups.

An older man enters. He has graying hair and kind intelligent eyes. "Check her vitals. I'll be back in a few."

The younger men swab my cheek and take my temperature. They check my blood pressure. There are other tests I don't recognize. Beeps and scans and devices, all of which are alien to me. I take silent deep breaths, trying to stay calm.

The door opens, and a voice asks, "How is everything?"

"Her vitals are all within target, Dr. Cluney."

"Excellent. Ready the hectocotylus for insemination." I hear the structure whiz down, and I open my eyes to stare at it between my legs.

"And . . . drill."

I close my eyes again and try to stay calm as the machine starts to approach my vagina. I've survived this before, I think. Once, at least. How many other times? It starts to bore into me. I chew the inside of my mouth until I taste blood and detach from my body, imagining myself as a weightless balloon drifting away from the rest of my bunch. Suddenly, the grating stops. My mind screams in the silence, afraid of what could be next.

"Sorry to interrupt."

I am so grateful I could cry.

"What is it?"

"This one needs to go out to the Gunks."

"What do you mean? She's already done two rounds of insemination. Results are due from the Hole any moment now."

"Yes, I am aware, but she has become a risk." Saje has an edge in her voice.

"What about my risk? I'll be losing months of research!"

"It can't be helped, David. I wish it wasn't necessary, but she has been spoiled."

"And if the results are positive?" His question lingers in the air for a long moment, Saje apparently thinking it over.

"If it's positive, we may still need to start over with another. That'll be up to Victor. But I can show you the footage from her mandala if you need it. Trust me when I say she can no longer be used. Focus on the others."

Dr. Cluney sighs in frustration.

"Dress her and bring her upstairs. Wilden is waiting with the car."

The two young men release me from the clamps and awkwardly dress me. I start to shake as they take me upstairs. What had my mandala shown before I forced it off? What happens to risks? On the street, one of the men waits with me. I can smell the horrible jasmine rot of the car already. The dark sedan goes over a speed bump, and the glare from the sun lifts for a second. I see Henry at the wheel, not Wilden.

Fuck this.

I run, forcing my legs to move as fast as they can, wincing through the chafing deep inside me. I hear steps behind me. The doctor. A dark shadow cuts me off from the left and suddenly I am on the ground. Pebbles break my skin as someone drags me over gravel. My bones bounce over tree roots before I am lifted and carried to the car. The door shuts, locks engaging immediately.

"I've got her," Henry says to someone on the phone.

We start moving.

The partition starts to slide up, dividing the space between us. I try to hold on but feel the jasmine's cloying scent shutting down branch after branch of my mind. We turn a corner and I see a street sign ahead. I almost make out the first word before the piano lid slams shut, shrouding me in darkness.

CHAPTER THIRTY

The night peels away. In its place, a familiar room.

Victor is sitting on the bed beside me, rolling up a blindfold and laying it on the pillow. He puts a hand to my forehead. "How did you sleep?" he asks.

I realize with a cold terror that my hands and legs are bound together under a heavy blanket and I am unable to speak.

"Calm down." He thrusts a finger to my lips to quiet my whimpering. "Before any decisions are made, I want to offer you a choice. It's a courtesy I don't extend to everyone."

He takes the gauze from my mouth, and I hiccup from gulping air too quickly. He watches me with mild distaste as if my unencumbered breathing is deeply unattractive. "How much do you know about what we're doing?"

"Something is happening to the girls," I mumble through bruised lips. I suddenly feel weak and stupid. "Something is happening to me," I say, correcting myself. My eyes fill with tears.

"Saje believes you're a risk because of what you know." He nods to a shadow behind him, and I notice her silhouette, framed in the darkness. "But I think you're an asset because of what you *are*. Your constitution, not to mention our investment in optimizing it, puts you in a unique position. I'd like to propose a partnership."

Saje comes forward now, bringing some papers with her. She hands them to Victor before retreating into the shadows.

He looks at me with curiosity. "Anna, do you want children?" he asks.

I stare at him, confused by the question.

"No?" He looks surprised.

"I guess it would depend," I say.

"Depend?"

"On the circumstances."

"What circumstances would those be?" he asks.

"Would I be able to support the child? Would I be alone?"

He nods. "All valid concerns. What about your body?"

"What about my body?" I ask, not understanding his question.

"You're not afraid of the changes? The weight gain. The lasting effects. Stretch marks and cellulite?"

"I haven't thought about it too much," I say truthfully.

Victor's lips pull wide, and his teeth glow with the regular use of Holistik's bioluminescent phytoplankton toothpaste. "We've been working for years to develop a truly extraordinary procedure. At Apothecare, you became one of the chosen few who got to try this new technology. I call it Everlasting. It's a treatment that will revolutionize every woman's life. It's also the crown jewel of my career and a love letter, of sorts, to my mother."

I remain silent.

"More concretely, it's a hybridization that would result in a shorter pregnancy and absolutely no change in a woman's body. Pre- *or* postnatal."

"Hybrids. So, like a cross between . . . what?" I ask.

"We've tried many things over the years. With your batch, we finally hit upon the right mix, so to speak. We managed to get it so that by year two, the child will be fully human with no discernible differences from a normal toddler. We grow and monitor them in a specialized environment with a volunteer such as yourself, and hand them over to their parents."

I can hear my heartbeat in my ears, loud and erratic. When had I ever volunteered?

"It pained me to see you struggling with the financial burden of caring for your parents, so I created opportunities for you."

Everything is happening too quickly and too slowly at the same time. Victor is still speaking, turning the pages in his hand. He breaks a seal on the second page, and I recognize the packet of documents he is holding. He reaches in his suit jacket for something. A blue ballpoint pen. I watch as the pen moves from his left hand to my right hand.

(a) Volunteer agrees that all processes and products Volunteer is exposed to are confidential and may not be divulged in any manner whatsoever by Volunteer to any third parties . . .

I read the first sentence a few times, unable to focus on its meaning. Saje appears next to Victor, a manicured talon curling over his shoulder. "The results are in, Victor," she says, shaking her head. "It's not what we hoped."

"Oh." Victor looks puzzled. He pulls the unsigned papers from me.

"Wait—" I cry as he covers my nose and mouth with a cloth. I taste the jasmine on my tongue before losing consciousness.

Professor Zsaborsky lets me in on his way out. "It's been a while, hasn't it?" Victor says. Someone has wheeled a monolithic piano into Holistik. "Please," he says as he gestures at the instrument. I sit down at the bench and put my hands on the keys. "No, not there . . . here." He lifts me easily, as if I'm still a child, and seats me on the closed lid. I look around, taking everything in. The soft ceiling is pitted and slightly damp. Every so often, water drips onto my head. The curtains hang in the dead air like bodies. Floral incense in the room presses down on me. Pollen drifts into my lungs, ossifying. Victor's face looms over my own, his chin stretching downward in far-reaching strands like a mobile made of skin. He moves up and down over me. I try to reach up, to feel the texture of his skin, but I don't know where my hands are. I don't feel connected to them at all.

CHAPTER THIRTY-ONE

P lease," I gasp as someone chokes me. A terrible mix of baby powder and perspiration clogs my nostrils. I push the arm from my throat, surprised by how easily it lifts, unresponsive and cold to the touch. I start panicking, tearing my way through the pile of girls I am under, all seemingly asleep or unconscious, with gruesome abnormalities. A cough becomes an emptying of pale yellow liquid, forcing its way out of me. We are outside on a rocky dirt-covered path, all of us covered in a sticky paste that dazzles in the moonlight. I circle them, unable to believe what I see. One woman's skin is stippled like she's been emptied and filled with stones. There is hair everywhere—bunches of dirty, unevenly cut hair all over the girls. One of them sits up, covered in a hideous dripping caul. Her protruding eyes open and blink, a black substance leaking out of them.

"Astrid?" I whisper.

She stares at me for a few moments before lying back down. Her head makes a dull crack as it lands on the girl beneath her. I glimpse black bangs slashing across a white face and feel sick. Ants are crawling from swollen lips to a bloodless neck.

Lilith.

I am still trying to disentangle her from the others when I hear it. Beneath the throaty hush of stirring trees, I hear the nagging bass of uneven footsteps on sand. Something heavy is being dragged. Helpless, I abandon Lilith in the pile. She hits the other girls stiffly, already gone. I run away from the direction of the footsteps and end up somewhere above the girls. Three figures approach, dragging other bodies behind them. Saje's normally fiery hair is dull in the pale sunlight. Victor has a mask on, his brows wrinkled in distaste. He is carrying a meditation pillow with him, setting it down away from the pile. He gestures at Saje and Henry, who lift and position the girls. A giant bird suddenly lands on one of the large branches hemming us in from the cliff's edge. I feel the winds around me shifting. More are on their way.

At the first sound of wings fluttering, I turn away. I can't bear to watch. There has to be something I can do, but it is so isolated and remote here. No one will arrive in time. The sun is starting to rise. Victor is sitting cross-legged on his cushion with a peaceful expression on his face. I look from him to the pile of bodies, wincing as light reflected from a colossal mirror above me pierces my eyes. I gaze up at it. Strong direct sunlight is pouring onto me, causing me to feel dizzy. I can notice my sweat starting to steam. I am looking at a modernized excarnation structure, modeled after the ones used by the Zoroastrians.

I start running from the pillar of light. My legs carry me higher. The lens is mounted on a massive vertical hinge. I see the light cascading in waves from each concentric circle. I get behind the lens, so I am hidden from view, and start to push it down, angling it away from the bodies and onto the standing figures. It is so heavy that it takes all of my strength, and even then, it moves too slowly. The back of the lens is scalding, the heat raising blisters from my skin. I watch my right hand blur, the skin pooling between the fingers. I cry out. For agonizing seconds, I endure the pain, seemingly to no effect. Finally, the heat starts to shimmer as it concentrates around them. They turn to the lens. Saje is pointing at me with a controller in her hand. I feel the mirror turning up, slipping from my grasp. I press harder, my entire body now on the back of the mirror. I can feel the tears evaporating from my face as the top layer of my skin starts to simmer.

The first thing to catch fire is Victor's mask. Then Saje's hair, finally becoming as red as she's always wanted. Henry stands dumbfounded, looking at them with shock, not realizing his own pants have started to singe until the hardware of his belt brands him. He starts bucking, burning his hands while undoing the clasp. The birds inch closer, turning their heads and fluttering their wings in excitement.

I have to peel myself from the back of the lens. The skin on my hands moves like a fluid. I scream when I see a hint of white bone exposed. Victor starts screaming, too, farther down below, as the flames lick his face. A horrific sound as the fire crawls inside him through his open mouth. Saje, her magnificent red hair now the entire length of her body, drops to the ground howling as her beloved birds watch. But fire only knows hunger and starts to catch on the heap. The women lie there, unmoving. *Get up!* I want to scream. *Run!*

I will my legs down the mountain, stumbling past the cages and into the house. I look frantically for a phone, finding only an old rotary one made of carved malachite.

"Please please please," I hear myself saying out loud. "Please."
I run for it, praying it works. That it isn't just decorative, like
everything else these fucking people care about.

I try not to look at my hands. Try to ignore the pain. Behind
the phone, a mirrored wall threatens to show what I can't bear
to see.

"Hello?"

"There's a fire! You have to come right now! Please!"

"Slow down. Where are you?"

"Farm. Organic Provisions farm. It's—"

I'm trying to think of how to describe it to her when I smell
the smoke. Flesh charred and burning, no longer outside but inside. Too close to me. I am looking down at my hands, to see if
they are the source, when I hear something behind me. Victor,
gasping through his new fire-laced lungs as he staggers toward
me. Around his neck, a ruff of flames. I don't have time to think.
I plunge my ruined hands through the fire to circle his neck with
the coiled telephone cable. It disintegrates instantly, the copper
wires underneath slashing through my flesh. I scream and try to
run, but he wraps his hands around my throat.

Maybe fire is discerning after all, I think as he lifts me off my
feet. It has consumed all the organic material on his face, everything that was inorganic to himself. For the first time, I see what
he looks like without the grafts that still drip from him like melting wax. I can almost tell where he might be from, the face, after
all, a history and path to be trod and traced. How ordinary he is.
What sunken cheeks, feeble jaw, and average features. For a brief
moment, before my eyes close, I think he looks more handsome
than he ever has.

CHAPTER THIRTY-TWO

A woman sets a tray down in front of me with orange slices, a porridge with cubes of dried fruit, and a small paper cup of milk. She leaves before I can thank her. I look around me. Heavy black curtains are pulled to the side and sunlight comes in greedily, licking at the edges of the furniture. Instinctively, I retreat from its grasp.

A TV is on, and a news reporter is speaking. "He has not been found, but old interviews have resurfaced that may give some insight into why Organic Provisions was engaging in illegal activity that ranged from testing dangerous products on humans to inseminating young women with animal sperm without their knowledge."

I shudder at Victor's voice and close my eyes.

"I want to solve the great mysteries of our time," he says from the TV. "How to be beautiful. How to live forever. Not everyone will agree with the methods I'm willing to try to get there. But not everyone deserves to be beautiful."

"Now it's clear who Victor Carroll thought deserved to be beautiful: those who could afford it. Holistik, the pioneer in 'clean beauty,' among other trends in the natural beauty and wellness space, was testing on animals as well as young women to perfect the services offered to their wealthy clientele. Young women have come forward from just about every industry claiming someone, often Victor himself, offered monetary support in exchange for procedures or experiments they can't remember. A seizure of Organic Provisions documents shows a diabolical system exploiting young women he groomed and/or drugged under false pretenses. Footage confiscated from the offices of his company RealSight shows a disturbing amount of surveillance monitoring the mostly female staff employed at various Holistik locations. More on this story as it develops. Reporting live from New York, this is Jacqueline Peña."

When I lift the cup of milk to my lips, I notice my hands look different. No nails in sight, just slabs of flesh. I take a sip, put the cup back down, and examine them more closely. I try to shake them out. There is a thin layer of something translucent between the bottoms of my right hand's fingers. A papery fabric I can't move. I use my left hand to try and peel the layer off, but that hand is also stuck together. I sit up, frustrated now, and that's when I feel the change. My body is slow to respond, rebounding on itself. I lift the covers with my glued hands and see a body I don't recognize. Slightly green with patches of hair all over it. And skin. So much excess skin.

The woman comes back to collect the food tray. Mostly full. My appetite decreased sharply after seeing myself. I try to figure out what I should say to her. What question to start with.

"Excuse me?" My lips flop as I speak, feeling swollen, and my voice is so guttural there is barely a pitch to it. I don't sound too different from the branches outside that are scratching at the windowpanes.

She stares at me for a moment, speechless, before running out of the room.

Time passes and she still doesn't return. I continue to assess my body, not knowing what to make of it, and too afraid to search for a mirror. I look at my arms closely in the sunlight. The color of my skin is beautiful if I forget it is supposed to be skin. A light lime color, pocked and lined with rivulets, dark blue veins running through everything. I hear a voice in my head: *She has been spoiled.* I tentatively reach up to feel my face. There, too, is excess flesh. My hair is brittle and ragged, crumbling in my fingers if I rub too hard. Gone is the thick swath of smooth coiling hair. Anxiety gnaws at my stomach. Surely this is just another one of my bad dreams. The nurse forgot the food tray in her surprise, so I line up the finished orange peels. They look like open palms. I stretch my arms and move my wrists, bending them forward and backward. Try to get used to my new hands with the rind of gossamer wrapped around them.

I know that voice.

"They're a huge company! I assumed everyone they brought in had consented. Otherwise, I would have had nothing to do with the place. After all, we take an oath as doctors. I dedicated my life to researching Everlasting. That was a poor choice of words . . . I meant my life's work. Thirty-five years down the drain."

"Back to you, Michelle."

A nurse sits in a corner under the TV, knitting something.

"Where am I?" I ask her.

"You're awake!"

The nurse stands abruptly and turns off the TV. A deep silence asserts itself, as if the room is filling with a dense heavy fog.

"Where am I?" I ask again. I bring my hands out from under the covers. Both are still webbed. With despair, I try to separate them but can't.

"Take it easy, take it easy." The nurse tries to shush and calm me.

"What happened?"

"You were found at a farm. Do you remember being at the farm?"

I don't say anything.

"You had a pretty bad concussion, so it makes sense that you can't recall."

"My hands."

"There was a fire. Do you remember the fire?"

"And my body?" I croak.

She sits down beside me and puts a warm hand on my cheek.

"You were taking a lot of pills and supplements at your former workplace. They caused violent changes in your body, and when you stopped taking them, your body was left on its own to regulate the volatile substances. It's a terrible tragedy and it'll take some time to get used to things, but you are by far one of the luckier ones." She smiles and squeezes one of my crimped hands. "Besides, you're a hero. Try to get some rest."

Only the slow gathering of shadows in the room gives me any indication that time is passing. I fall asleep eventually and wake to my useless paws scratching music on the blank sheets. I had dreamed of my parents, and their concerned faces shine for a moment before fading away. My head is encrusted in the salt of dried tears. I decide to try and get out of bed. It is difficult. There is a lot more body to negotiate, but I am already getting used to not having the full range of my hands. My feet are soft with disuse, like fresh dinner rolls. I check to make sure they are actually standing on the ground. The skin between my toes is also stretched and scabbed over, feet bound together, a regression of my people by hundreds of years, and a return to my name.

I slowly walk to the bathroom, holding on to as much as I can. My new abundance moves lazily around me like a body of water. In the bathroom, looking at my reflection, more shock. I touch the mirror, remembering the last one I saw.

CHAPTER THIRTY-THREE

t takes many months, but eventually, I am able to return to a semblance of normal life. There is no regenerating what has been lost, but I can move without great difficulty, cook, eat, and take care of myself. I don't walk as much as I undulate, and I use the many crevices and pocks of my body to hold what my hands would have once held. I am just as compelling as before, but in a way that makes people keep their distance. Everywhere I go, people look away, their faces streaked with alarm and sympathy. Children often run or scream when they see me. One little boy pointed a finger at his mother and hollered at the top of his lungs, "Liar! You told me monsters weren't real!" It's unfortunate that I can undermine months of parental reassurance in just a few seconds, but it's probably better for kids to learn early on that yes, monsters are real. They just don't look anything like you'd expect. I'm also surprised to discover I don't mind my new appearance. I enjoy the immense freedom that comes with being safe from desire. And it is a kind of power to embrace ugliness and its possibility of expression, so much more imaginative than beauty.

At Applebaum Care, I badge in to visit the woman now known, once again, as Sally Brown. The nurses here, so used to the aged and diseased, are among the only people who don't find me particularly interesting. I feel comfortable enough at Applebaum that I've started volunteering a few days a week. Through the veil of their rheumy eyes, the patients can't see that the hand comforting them is more flipper than paw.

Margot squelches down the hall and embraces me without reservation. I drink in her warmth and recognition, using them to calm my nerves.

"You sure about this?" she asks.

I nod slowly, though, truthfully, I am not sure about this.

From the doorway, I see her face reflected in the compact mirror she is holding. With a steady hand, she is applying a rich plum lipstick. She notices me in the doorway and waves me in.

"Is it you? Is that really you, darling?" She carefully adjusts her dark red wig. "What do you think?"

I had read about her reconstructive surgeries in a tabloid. The first thing she did when her lawyers won her freedom with a mental disorder defense. In the face of her angelic beauty, I have to remind myself of all the ugly things she has done. She looks the same, maybe even better. Much younger than her seventy-two years.

"Oh, just look at you." She gazes at me wistfully, though she is the one in a hospital bed. "It hurts me to see you this way. I'll give you the names of my surgeons, of course. And I can set the appointments up for you. They might be able to prioritize you with my referral. They're not cheap, but they're miracle workers, aren't they? Except with hair, which won't grow back." She fluffs her wig nervously. "Come closer. There's no need to be afraid of me. I don't blame you for anything."

My considerable body seethes with anger at her words.

"Why would you? You and Victor are to blame for everything," I surprise myself by saying.

Her eyes grow, astonished. "But you understand, don't you? Victor took advantage of me, too. Offered me beauty, power, a chance to change the world. No one would turn down what he gave me. Surely you can understand?"

"He gave you just enough power to take it from other women. It was transference, a distraction."

"I know that now. I can't explain it, but when it was all happening, I didn't feel like I had a choice. I was confused and then I was too involved. When we met, he saved my business. My life, even. And he supported my family. I believed in Holistik's original mission, but I also felt indebted to him. Suddenly we were in too deep, and it became impossible to find a way out." She looks ashamed for a moment before applying another layer of lipstick. "You haven't answered my question. What do you think of the surgeries?"

I want to cry. "Saje. Why? . . . Why me? Why Helen?"

An exasperated sigh as if she's sick of talking about the loss I've endured. "You should be grateful. We saved you, we made you from nothing! And not just you, but so many others from the ballet, the theater, the—what's the one with tumbling?" She smiles encouragingly at me, ticking them off with her fingers.

"But I quit. I was out of the Conservatory!" I search her eyes. "That night when we met at the restaurant. I know that wasn't an accident."

Her finger slips, and she rushes to conceal the dark smudge. "It wasn't."

I exhale slowly. "What about Henry? Was it a coincidence that I met him?"

"Of course not. E-ros isn't available to the public yet. Victor has sole control over who can see and download the beta. The algorithm was designed to eventually bring all targets to Henry."

I sputter in disbelief at the pride, the condescension in her voice.

"We badly needed test subjects for Everlasting. Creative intelligent women who would transmit those qualities to our projects. Victor was still keeping tabs on you, and with your parents more or less out of the way, it became very convenient to consider you as an option. All of our girls are somewhat isolated from any family or social circles for precisely this purpose."

"What did you do to me?" My voice shakes. Blue-black droppings have begun leaking out of me in bigger sizes, further developed. The other day, I discovered a fingernail among one of eight spiraling extensions.

"Ah." She sighs. "We were so close with you. If Everlasting had worked, we would have changed the world together. We would have set women free, given them the gift of choice. We just needed a few more—"

"A few more women to die? What about *our* choice?" My face is wet.

She glares at me. "What choice? Did you choose to be born with a womb? Something that pops out children even if you don't want them? No woman escapes pregnancy unscathed. No matter how wonderful they are, offspring gorge on our perfect bodies and alter them forever. I had a husband and children. Did he look at me after I got pregnant? Of course not. He left me disfigured and impoverished. If I hadn't met Victor then, I would have killed myself." She glares at me with her new eyes, ocular prosthetics she didn't need but chose to get. They're made of amethysts and diamonds that render her legally blind.

"And Helen?" I ask.

She looks sad for the first time. "That was never supposed to happen. She was just too kind. Befriended all the girls at the Gunks. Didn't know that we were testing new formulations on their supply."

The question I don't want to ask but need to: "Did Helen know anything?"

She stretches, her flabby upper arm skin the only visible sign of age. "Oh no. Or else she wouldn't have taken the same supply as the others. Her bedroom was filled with experimental products, which, we now know, were lethal. Victor was heartbroken. Helen was his favorite. Mine, too," she adds softly. "At least she was beautiful while it lasted. She was really very ordinary before Victor started assembling her."

I shudder with revulsion at the mention of Victor's name and at the beautiful woman in front of me whose involvement in predatory crimes is being presented in the media as lunacy and victimhood, ambition, even feminism.

"There was never any sex work, was there?" I almost feel relieved, asking. "Why even go through the trouble of pretending?"

"We needed you to sign forms that would give us express consent for physiological experiments. Sex work just seemed more plausible. Besides, there was sex, once. The first time."

I shake my head in disgust.

"It's a privilege to connect with someone at that level of

spiritual awareness. I was a nervous wreck before Victor started sleeping with me and transplanting his calm energy to my mind. And it's not like it was easy for Victor. He prefers sexual partners much younger than you and me. So he may be flawed in some ways, but his wellness stats are off the charts—"

"Flawed?" I ask with disbelief.

"Well, no one is perfect. But think of the good we do with Organic Provisions! The spiderwebs we use in our false lashes are being researched now for use in joint repair. It'll greatly benefit those who have suffered in military service and people like myself with arthritis. And you saw yourself! The way your eyes and skin color changed. That kind of beauty brings joy to all who see it. Power to those who have it."

I gather myself up to fit through the doorway. There is no reasoning with her.

She struggles to sit up taller, dropping her lipstick on the floor. "You'll . . . come back?"

As I look at her, something dawns on me. "That first time you brought me to the Gunks. I thought I had rolled off the bed, but you had dumped me there."

She looks at me with feigned confusion.

"You were going to kill me if I didn't wake up. Leave me to the birds."

"Darling, I couldn't be sure you weren't dead already. Wouldn't you want your body to be of use?"

I feel sick.

"You'll come back and visit me? There's no one else. I'm so lonely . . . and I'm afraid he will—" She examines the monitors and screens in the room before resuming her casual tone of voice.

"It's just you and me now. We're the only ones who went through it all. We need each other."

I look around the room, suddenly queasy with the idea that someone could be eavesdropping. I turn to leave.

"Wait! Look!" She brings her head down abruptly on one of the metal handrails lining the side of her hospital bed. A vibrant metallic sound twangs in the air. Her left cheek is slightly dented from the movement. "See? The skin is a metal hybrid! Impenetrable!"

I almost want to stay. Roll up my sleeves and test her supposed impenetrability, but pity has begun its slow climb from the bottom of my stomach.

"Goodbye, Sally."

CHAPTER THIRTY-FOUR

The fire becomes international news. Eventually, a documentary about Victor is released in seven parts.

The first episode examines his relationship with his mother. She was Victor's hero, a beautiful woman who was abused by her husband. She eventually fled, leaving Victor and his many siblings with an alcoholic father. They trace a line from his mother's constant pregnancies and eventual abandonment to Victor's obsession with dominance over women's bodies. His childhood was the perfect catalyst for Everlasting.

Girlfriends and ex-wives are interviewed in subsequent episodes about their tubal ligations. A broken man is given fifteen minutes to talk about his wife, an ex-employee at Holistik who died because she was made to carry her hybrid to term.

"We would never have traveled to this state if we had known the baby would come so early. And when it became clear—oh god—that it wasn't mine or even hers . . . we tried to tell them it wasn't human. They didn't care." I recognize her name. There aren't, in my experience, too many people named Cassandrea. Dr. Cluney makes an appearance despite being in jail. There is a bonus feature that focuses on the relationship between Victor and Henry, who fled and is yet to be found. I had declined to participate in the documentary, but there is a brief segment about me. They focus on my Chinese descent, making me a trope, as if to say only an exotic dragon lady could have been the one to set fire to Victor's house of cards.

I watch it all in one night. Sucked in by the high production value, I almost forget that it's a story that has greatly affected me. I almost feel sorry for Victor. I certainly understand him better. Music also requires an absolute commitment to aesthetics.

Surprisingly, almost an entire episode is dedicated to Alice, who is not only my old roommate but also, apparently, my best friend. "I could totally tell something was off about the whole place. There was just a stink whenever she came home, you know? It kept getting stronger and stronger. I actually did a powerful cleanse on her once and it worked for a while, but she was being re-exposed every day. I can't help people who won't help themselves."

"And Holistik? Did you ever go?"

"I did. I was invited to do an appraisal, and what a horror show. Misery and pain screaming from every surface. I've never been surrounded by so much agony. The products were literally filled with grief. I mean, now we know, like, *literally* literally."

Here, I pause the episode to remember how eagerly Alice applied all that grief to her face and asked for samples of more. But maybe I should have taken her more seriously the day of her unwelcome visit. She did try to warn me.

"And tell us, what's next for you?"

"Well, of course, my memoir will be out in just a few short

months. Very excited about that. I'm also thrilled to be accepting the position of director of provenance remediation at Sotheby's."

"Congratulations! Sotheby's! What will that job entail?"

"I mean, it's Sotheby's, right? So everything up for auction has pristine documentation, but for those items where the origins or papers may be slightly in dispute, I'll be in charge of exorcising any history."

I can almost hear Charlie in the background, weakly bleating "babe" with pride.

I have become a celebrity, too. People secretly delight in my transformation. On the TV in the waiting room before a therapy session, I see before and after photos of me. I focus on the now famous before photo, a girl with billowing hair and pale luminous skin, looking back at the camera with an endlessly lashed eye.

The Gunks farm is gone except for a giant mirror cracked in the dried overgrown grass. The Holistik franchise was bought by an unknown entity and became more successful than ever, largely due to the global media attention incited by the documentary.

Every year, around the time of my birthday, I find a letter from my "biggest fan" pushed under the door. The author begs me to consider various surgeries. Of the many that are mentioned, de-syndactylization is the only one that tempts me.

Don't you miss playing Mozart?

The envelope always smells like fresh flowers just beginning to burn. There is never a return address. Every time, I rip up the letter and feed it to the fire.

As far as I know, no one else has heard from Victor, though every few years someone claims to have seen him, leading to renewed media interest. Of course, with the money and technology he has at his disposal, he could look like anyone or anything at this point. I still don't know how I survived. When the memories come back to me, I can only remember his hands closing on my throat.

Wherever he is, he must be ugly. I remember his limited perception of beauty when we discussed music, applying it only to Haydn and Bach, and think he must believe himself too hideous to be seen. Why else would he have stayed hidden when he has the money and powerful network to cobble together a new existence for himself? He doesn't have the strength I have, given to me by my parents. Music, which has always privileged being heard above being seen. I look in the mirror and flinch, but I don't look away. The music I love teaches me there is no real beauty without ugliness.

The sleek labs of Genysis in Witch's Hole State Park have been abandoned. Now overrun with wild animals, it has come full circle for a place that claimed to renature what had been denatured.

Years from now, when they develop shiny condominiums over the Gowanus Canal, they'll unearth the cathedral of Apothecare, half sunk in the brackish water and stinking of leaf rot and melting metal. Within the wild marsh, only the golden room is recognizable. The beeswax pillars, though nibbled by salt, are still largely intact, hulking above a cork floor swollen with coal tar. I often dream of returning.

I look barely human, and yet I've never felt more myself. I am as undefinable, as *other*, as music. If I can't look like my parents, I don't want to look like anyone.

The rind around my hands thickens with inactivity, so I've started playing piano again. Just to keep them moving. I learn the Ryabov by ear, often layering my hands over Ba's recording. It often surprises people to learn that the piano is a percussion instrument. There is an implied violence to percussion not typically associated with piano. Especially after the Cultural Revolution, Ba must have felt even more connected to an instrument that needs the strike of a finger to sound. I try to believe that what I have lost is necessary for some new phrase, yet unheard, that only I can compose.

I try to apply what my parents taught me, but my hands are so different that I must develop a new piano technique. I upload videos to YouTube, and they start going viral. Thousands and eventually millions of views. People want to see the girl who plays with hands like beaks. Since everything about me at the piano is wrong and ugly, I lose all pressure to fit my sound into the conventional beauty of classical music. Now I can try to play Adès and Britten and Crumb the way I want to hear them. Not as pieces but as experiences. Instead of emulating great pianists, I try to sound like worms exulting in damp earth, birds squawking in the jungle at night, the soft pour of moonlight on pavement. I wish I could tell my parents I'm a famous pianist now, that I have achieved their American dream. It only took a gimmick and cost me nearly everyone I know.

I'm not stupid. I know people watch my videos on mute, for the spectacle. Not to hear me, but to see the epoxied stumps with which I still try to express the ineffable. I know, and still, I play.

I had been afraid, at first, to continue without my parents. Now I know I have to keep playing. I am the throat by which my parents are sung and sustained.

I keep the photograph of us above the piano and play for them. It sits next to the ceramic Helen made for me, all those years ago. I see them in my dreams all the time. Ma. Baba. Lilith. Helen. Lilith's eyes gleam from where she stands in the back corner. She's too restless to sit down. Helen wants to be support-ive, so she sits in the front row, not realizing her hair is sucking up all the stage lighting. My parents sit upstairs in the very back row. I can almost make out their faces. They don't think their clothes are good enough and, anyway, they are late, coming from so far away. They never speak to me or clap at the end, but once in a while, I hear them singing along and I know I'm getting something right.

ACKNOWLEDGMENTS

I am grateful for so many people in my life, and one of the most wonderful things about writing a book is having a physical object to give them, which has in writing how much they mean to me.

Kirby Kim, I'll never be able to thank you enough for how much you have changed my life. My deepest gratitude to you for taking a chance on me.

Eloy Bleifuss Prado, this book would not be what it is without your many insightful reads. Thank you for your time and dedication.

Nathaniel Alcaraz-Stapleton, thank you for your hard work on my behalf.

I am so grateful to be a part of the Janklow and Nesbit family.

Pilar Garcia-Brown, my brilliant editor—the surgeon whose incisiveness revealed more heart and unclogged every artery—thank you for making me my best self. From the moment I met you and John Parsley, I felt supported and excited about the fun we would all have together. I am so thankful for you both and for the rest of my wonderful team at Dutton. It is incredibly humbling to work with you all.

Lisset Lanza, thank you for your commitment and crucial assistance. It has been a pleasure working with you.

Mary Beth Constant, I am in awe of you. Thank you for lending your razor-sharp eyes in service of my book.

Alice Dalrymple, thank you for overseeing and coordinating so many moving parts.

Kaitlin Kall, thank you for making *Natural Beauty* more beautiful than I could have ever dreamed.

Amanda Walker and Lauren Morrow, I am so lucky to have such a fierce publicity team. Thank you for shouting me from the rooftops.

Stephanie Cooper and Nicole Jarvis, my heartfelt thanks for everything you have done to put this book out into the world.

Thank you, Jasmine Lake, for being an early reader and believer in my work. I am so excited that, because of you, *Natural Beauty* will reach even more audiences on screen. I feel incredibly lucky to be working with you and Mitchell Gomes at the United Talent Agency.

Thank you to everyone who gave me work in New York. Especially, Henry Wang, Pauline Kim, James Blachly, and Jessica McJunkins. You sustained me during the writing of this book, and it would not have been possible without you. I'm also grateful to every person I met freelancing. What a warm world we made together.

I am so grateful for the orchestras that have welcomed me again and again. Thank you, Jenny Ross, first and foremost for your friendship and for bringing me to be a part of the ProMusica Chamber Orchestra, a musical environment like nothing I have experienced before. I am so grateful for my ProMusica hosts as well, Angela and John Petro, whose beautiful upstairs apartment

I often used as a writing/editing retreat between rehearsals and concerts.

Thank you Lady Adelle Eslinger-Runnicles, Sir Donald Runnicles, and everyone in my Grand Teton Music Festival family. This place has meant the world to me and has healed me in ways I can only hope to express one day. Much of the music writing in this book was inspired by moments I had onstage here.

And thank you, Richard Brown, for being the first to welcome me. I owe so much to you and Susan for your care and friendship.

There are many educators I am indebted to . . .

The Cavani Quartet (Annie Fullard, Mari Sato, Kirsten Docter, and Merry Peckham), who were my coaches in 2003, 2004, and 2005 at the Encore School for Strings. Working with four of the most inspiring, dynamic, and passionate women I have ever met was galvanizing and formative. Nothing short of magical. I wouldn't be a musician without those coachings.

Merry, when I was thirteen, you turned to me when we were walking outside and told me I had a good soul. I always remember that moment as one of the first in my life when I didn't feel worthless. Thank you.

Susan McClary, you were one of the first people who made me think there was anything of value in my mind. You changed the course of my life. So did your Beethoven Quartets class. Thank you for believing in me, for treating me like an equal to your formidable mind, and for being yourself. You have changed everything about the field of classical music, and we are better for it.

Paul Kantor, I am forever indebted to you for being my mentor. Your fierce intellect, endless curiosity, wisdom, deep consideration, and playfulness inform everything I do. Thank you for teaching me, for committing to seeing me once a week for twelve years. That commitment radically altered my life. You saw me at my proudest moments, as well as my most shameful. I have been many people in the past couple of decades, many of whom I am not proud of, but you continued to open the door for me and to accept me with love and grace through everything. You taught me how to question things, how to see who people can be and what they need to get there. I continue to learn from you every day. When I practice, I hear your voice in my head. When I teach, I find myself saying things you've said to me. I am so grateful for the years you spent leading me to the self you knew was there all along.

Amanda Vernon, I'll never forget our many conversations about books and writing. Thank you for always taking me to bookstores and libraries and lending me so many books of your own. I was so lucky to find such a deeply intelligent and gentle friend in you.

My friends. What would I do without you? Cassandra Jackson, Dorothy Ro, Jennifer Johnson, Jen Liu, Kelsey Williams, Liz Weber, Michi Theurer, you were my biggest supporters and believers throughout the writing of this book, and I couldn't have done it without you. Thank you for inspiring me endlessly. I love you.

I am deeply thankful for my family.

My grandmother. Who said wherever I went, she wanted to go. Thank you for being with me, Nainai.

My sister-in-law, Sarah. Thank you for taking care of me in every way. For always feeding me the most delicious Korean food and for supporting me 1,000 percent. I am so lucky to count you—and, by extension, Jackie and Brent—as family. It is a joy and a privilege to watch the way you are raising Amelia and Ellie to be strong, incredible humans.

My brother, Frank, thank you for being one of my favorite people and violinists. I am far from alone in having you as a hero and it has always been an honor to try to fill your shoes. It remains a life goal of mine to make art that is as meaningful as yours is to me.

Thank you, Johanan Ottensooser, for being the love of my life. Without you, nothing would be possible. Thank you for nourishing me in every possible way. For being full of love and energy and positivity. You bring so much joy and light to my life. Boba and I are the luckiest creatures in the world to wake up to life with you every day.

Thank you, Mama and Baba. You came here with nothing but somehow managed to give me everything. If I accomplish anything, it is because of you. I am an extension of your achievements and all I have ever wanted to do with my life is make you proud.

DISCUSSION QUESTIONS

1. The narrator faces classism and racism during her time at the Conservatory. How do her experiences there compare and contrast to her job at Holistik?

2. Holistik is full of strange, unsettling, and invasive procedures, but they are believable extensions of the modern beauty world. What is the most unusual procedure you've heard of in real life and what did you think about it?

3. On page 82, the narrator says to Helen: "Beauty has always been one of the only ways women have been able to access power, and I can't fault any of them for wanting more of it." How do you feel about this?

4. How do you think people can determine the line between self-care and self-destruction?

5. Victor doesn't only work to promote mainstream beauty standards. He also invests in obscure, nontraditional alterations, like horse tails and crocodile skin. "He may not agree with other definitions of beauty, but he certainly wants to profit from them." (p. 129) What do you think this says about the relationship between culture and counterculture?

6. How does the narrator's understanding of her sexuality develop over the course of the novel? How do you think she understands it at the end of the book?

7. There are many parallels between music and appearance in the book. On page 153, the narrator thinks: "I didn't find it very interesting to practice solely beautiful music. Beauty only reaches so far. . . . At the end of the day, it was when composers tried to grasp something at the edge of beauty, or just past it, that made the most meaningful and challenging music to work on." Do you agree?

8. When the narrator first starts at Holistik, she believes she may be a "diversity hire." Later, she learns many of the other staff are also women of color, despite their appearances. How does the narrator's understanding of race, culture, and identity change over the novel?

9. Victor and his staff claim that using nature—both organic products and live animals—makes their products inherently more moral. How have you seen this occur in real life and what do you think about it?

10. "I am the throat by which my parents are sung and sustained." (p. 251) Discuss the narrator's relationship with her parents.

11. There is a contrast in the book between the bodily changes caused by nature, such as age and pregnancy, and the changes made by beauty products and procedures. What do you think are the differences in the ways these change people?

12. "And it is a kind of power to embrace ugliness and its possibility of expression, so much more imaginative than beauty." (p. 239) What do you think of this line?

ABOUT THE AUTHOR

LING LING HUANG is a writer and violinist. She plays with several ensembles, including the Oregon Symphony, Grand Teton Music Festival Orchestra, ProMusica Chamber Orchestra, and Experiential Orchestra, with whom she won a Grammy Award in 2021. *Natural Beauty* is her first novel.